W9-BEC-684

02/2016

DRIVEN

Kelley Armstrong

ILLUSTRATIONS BY XAVIÈRE DAUMARIE

SUBTERRANEAN PRESS 2016

First Edition

ISBN
978-1-59606-757-8

Subterranean Press
PO Box 190106
Burton, MI 48519

subterraneanpress.com

Prologue

"FUCK THIS SHIT," Clay muttered as he surveyed the landscape. He might have been referring to the immediate situation, but those three words summed up everything about this predicament. Two months ago Malcolm Danvers had called to tell us he'd killed two mutts who'd been after our kids. He didn't want a thank you or any other reward. He wanted back into the Pack.

Malcolm Danvers. The guy who'd made his son's— Jeremy's—life a living hell. The guy who went into self-imposed exile when Jeremy beat him in the Alpha race. For over twenty years, we'd thought Malcolm was dead. Then he turned up, a bigger sociopath than ever. One we could not kill. Could not even catch. Round and round we went, until Malcolm himself said, "Fuck this shit." And, "I want back in."

Let him back into the Pack, he said. Where we could keep an eye on him. Where he'd be a threat only to our enemies.

With that, he put me in the worst predicament I'd faced as Alpha. An unwinnable situation.

Fuck this shit, indeed.

I was here to let Malcolm know our decision. "Here" was Bulgaria, where he'd been, first in self-imposed exile and then under my orders to stay in one place and as far from us as possible.

Malcolm said he'd chosen a forest clearing, with enough open space that we could talk without constantly glancing over our shoulders, anticipating attack. That's what was before me. And yet…

It was an almost perfectly cleared sphere, like a crop circle in the middle of a forest, with no crops for miles. It looked ritualistic. That was what had our hackles rising, as if by stepping into this circle, we'd accidentally summon a demon. Which wasn't far off from the truth. Except for the "accident" part. We *had* summoned this particular demon.

"We know he hates magic," Clay said.

True. He only partnered with other supernaturals when the Nast Cabal forced him to, and he'd usually killed them before the job began.

"Power is tooth and claw and fist for Malcolm," Clay continued. "Anything else is cowardice."

Also true. That's one reason he hates Jeremy—because he has other powers, more mystical ones.

I peered around. "Which means there's zero chance this is a ritual circle that will incinerate us the moment we step into it."

"*Zero* might be pushing it."

I glanced over at Clay. He shrugged. As my mate and my beta, his job is to be truthful with me. Which he is, even when I'd really rather he wasn't.

We surveyed the clearing again. It was about a hundred feet wide, and completely flat, leaving no room for anyone to hide. A table with two chairs incongruously waited in the center of it. As we watched from the edge, a man walked out from the tree line. Broad-shouldered, powerful build, graying hair. Malcolm is in his eighties, but a combination of a werewolf's slow aging, a lifelong attention to his health and some Cabal cryogenics experiments means he's no weak old man. Unfortunately.

Malcolm pulled out one of the chairs, sat, folded his hands on the table and waited. He didn't look my way. He knew where I was—I wasn't hiding. He just waited.

"Give me a reason not to go over there," I whispered to Clay.

"I can give you fifty why we shouldn't even be here."

When I turned toward him, he sighed, ran his hand through his short curls and then sighed again.

"Fuck," he said. "I'm sorry. I just—"

"I know."

"This is the only solution. We both agreed. Jeremy agreed. Hell, you're the one who wanted to do this the *least*, so I have no right to complain now that we're here."

I said nothing.

"I hate this," he said finally.

"We all hate this."

But the only alternative was to tell Malcolm to stick his request up his ass, and let him keep killing anyone who got in his way. Just continue chasing him, and pray I didn't lose any of my Pack doing it, because we'd already come close to that more than once.

No. This was the only solution. And it burned because of that. Burned so bad. I'd failed to bring him down, and so it had come to this.

"It's about taking control," said a voice behind me. "Not giving in."

I looked over my shoulder as Nick stepped out of the woods, where he'd been patrolling. He came up behind me and put his arms around my waist and I let myself lean back against him, relaxing for a split second before I straightened.

"He came to us," Nick said. "To you. A female Alpha. In asking for it, he had to admit you're in charge. That you have the job he once wanted more than anything. I might not have managed to kill him, but you beat him down to this. Coming to us with his tail between his legs."

Fine words. Empowering words, and I loved Nick for them. But Malcolm never put his tail between his legs. This was just another move in his chess game.

"I know you don't want her alone out there," Nick said to Clay. "But if he vaulted across the table, she'd see him coming, and she's good enough to take him down."

"Hmmm," I said doubtfully.

"At the very least you're good enough to hold him off until Clay can take him down. Which is all you need to be, because Clay will fly across that field at the first sign of trouble."

"You've taken him down before," Clay said. "You're a match for him. Hell, even..." He glanced at Nick.

"I appreciate that you actually didn't finish that sentence," Nick said.

"Didn't need to."

Nick flipped him the finger, but it was good-natured. Nick would be the first to admit he isn't the Pack's best fighter. He doesn't want to be. But he had taken on Malcolm and sent him running. I'd taken him on and put him down. I just had to remind myself that those victories didn't guarantee one here. We could never underestimate Malcolm. We'd done it too often.

A man slipped through the trees to our left. He stopped and motioned to me. It was Andrei, one of the Russian

Pack. The Bulgarian Pack had refused to let me bring more than two of my wolves into their territory. The Russians announced that they had four wolves who really wanted to vacation in Bulgaria, and would the Alpha mind? Of course the Bulgarian Alpha knew exactly what was going on. But his was a small Pack in a small country, and the Russians were neither. So four Russian wolves were scouring the forest under my orders.

Malcolm rose from the table and said, his voice echoing across the open clearing, "You can call off your Ruskie hounds, Elena. I didn't bring backup. I don't need it."

He emphasized the "I" in that last sentence, and Clay growled under his breath.

"He's taunting you," Nick said. "Trying to get you onto the playing field before you've done a thorough sweep."

"I know." I motioned for Andrei to finish his search. It took another fifteen minutes. Then he came out and said the forest was clear.

"We will take our positions and watch," he said. "Удачи."

My knowledge of Russian was still rudimentary, but I knew that word, having heard it from Roman Novikov—the Alpha—and every Russian wolf helping me on this mission. Удачи. *Good luck.*

I started across the clearing. Clay followed at my shoulder, a half-step behind. When we were twenty paces from the table, he stopped. I continued until I was close enough to touch my chair. Then I said, "Stand."

"But I brought chairs. And a table. Can you imagine the trouble I went through to get them into the Bulgarian forest?" Malcolm twisted and poked the back of his. "I even got padded ones, so you'll be comfortable. I'm guessing we'll be here a while."

"Stand."

He let out a deep sigh. "I understand you feel the need to exert your power over me, Elena. Might I point out that if you actually *had* that power, you wouldn't need to prove it? And that you embarrass yourself with these petty displays?"

"So that's a no?"

"If you insist on me standing, then I will, but understand that it's only to humor you. And the fact you've had to ask multiple times proves you aren't really Alpha material."

"No," I said. "It proves you aren't really Pack material. I wasn't telling you to stand to exert dominance. I wanted you on your feet where I can see your hands, and where you can do the same for me. I wasn't making a point; you were. You stayed sitting to prove that you still have the power."

I put my hands on the table and leaned toward him. "You did not consider, even for one second, that I might have a valid reason for asking. As a Pack wolf, you're supposed to trust I have a valid reason, and as a recruit, you had the right to ask that reason. You just ignored me. That's why, Malcolm, the answer is no. You are not getting into the Pack."

His lips twitched. "And you came all this way to tell me that? No. You're like every other woman who finds herself in a position of power. You're always looking for an insult, and the minute you think you see one? Instead of fighting back, you withdraw in a snit. 'Sorry, Malcolm, but I never had any intention of letting you into my Pack. I just traveled thousands of miles and called in a favor with a foreign Pack for fun.'"

"Mmm, no. Not for fun. Although, yes, this next part *will* be fun." I lowered my voice. "Do you really think you're walking out of here alive, Malcolm?"

He blinked. That's all he did, but it was enough to make me smile and straighten.

"Oh, now you see," I said. "I didn't get pissy and dismiss you. I set you up. Double-crossed you. And that's what you didn't expect. Because no matter what you think of me, you expected at least one thing: honor." I stepped back. "Honor doesn't protect my Pack and my children. I brought you here to kill you, Malcolm."

I waved to my sides, and the three other Russian wolves stepped from the forest—two on my right, and Andrei and the other on my left. Nick stayed at the forest's edge behind me, with Clay between us.

"Blocked on three sides," I said. "But the fourth? The fourth is open. We're giving you a chance." I moved clear of the table and stopped right in front of him. "Run, Malcolm. Run as fast as you can."

He was close enough to grab me. To take me down. But he just rose and stood there. Seconds ticked by. Then he said, "No."

"I don't think you have a choice."

"Yes, I do. I can run or I can refuse." He met my gaze. "I don't run. Ever."

I laughed. "Is your memory failing? I seem to recall you running from Nick a few years ago. Running as fast as you could."

"I wasn't running from him. I was leaving to avoid killing him. Yes, I threatened to, but as I've pointed out, I did not. Nor have I touched anyone from your Pack without being attacked first, and even then, I haven't done any lasting damage."

"Through sheer nobility. Not because you're past your prime and can't do any *lasting damage* to a real werewolf."

He rolled his shoulders, as if struggling not to rise to the bait. "I can still fight. I'll provide a map of shallow graves if you'd like the proof. But the point, Elena, is that I choose not to run. I choose to fight." He looked over my shoulder. "I'll fight Clayton."

I snorted. "Right. With a poisoned pin or other deadly trick up your sleeve. Not a chance."

"I have nothing up my sleeve." He started unbuttoning his shirt. "And to prove it, I'll honor the ancient Greeks and disrobe before we fight."

"You're not fighting—"

"Because you think I'll win?"

"Because I don't trust you to fight fair."

"But I will. Otherwise, I'd have to deal with you."

"Which is so much scarier?"

"It is if I kill your mate. Do you think I missed that flash of fury in your eyes when I even suggested fighting him? If I cheated, you'd kill me. No quick break of the neck either. I'm sure you cringe at what Clayton has done, the stories of him torturing mutts. You think you're better than that. You aren't. You're just different. He kills for a purpose, as a warning to others. Cold and methodical. If I cheated in a fight and killed him, what you'd do to me would make me beg for what he did to those mutts. And you'd enjoy every second of it."

"As much fun as it is to stand here and let you psychoanalyze me—"

"A fair fight. Without clothing, there's no way for me to trick him."

"Without a trick, there's no way for you to win."

He shrugged, and behind me, Clay said, "He doesn't care."

I glanced back. Yes, I looked away from Malcolm. That wasn't an accident, no more than stepping within reach was when I told him to run. I provided a chance for him to strike so we'd have the excuse to cut him down where he stood. But he didn't move a muscle.

He was fucking with us.

"Whatever," I muttered and started for the woods, as if I'd given up. I walked past Malcolm. Right past him, with Clay on the opposite side, too far to charge to my rescue. I put my back to Malcolm, giving him the chance, with one lunge, to snap my neck. And even though I was ready for that—muscles tensed for counter-attack—it still took every ounce of courage I had to put my back to him.

And still he did nothing. I took another couple of steps and then turned and called to Clay, "You want this?"

He nodded and started to undo his belt, dropping his gaze to the buckle, looking away from Malcolm as I turned aside again. Everyone else was fifty paces away. Malcolm could kill me, throw my body aside, run into the forest and be gone before anyone could catch him.

Malcolm didn't move.

I glanced over my shoulder to see Malcolm unbuttoning the rest of his shirt. Clay looked up and caught my eye. *Good enough?* he was asking. With sincere reluctance, I nodded.

I walked back to Malcolm. "You can stop undressing. There isn't going to be a fight."

He twisted toward me as I approached. "I won't run, Elena. No matter what you—"

"You get your wish," I said. "You're in the Pack."

Something flickered across his face. Not a look of self-satisfaction, pleased that I'd capitulated. It almost seemed like disappointment. Then he said, carefully, "That was…a test?"

"I said I don't care about honor. I don't. What I care about is my Pack, and being the kind of leader they expect. Which is not the kind of leader who'd break her word to a former Pack member, even a psychopathic piece of shit like you."

I'd known he wouldn't run. What I'd wanted him to do was attack me. I'd given him increasingly better opportunities, hoping he'd provide the excuse I needed to kill him. And, damn him to hell, he had not.

"Sit," I said. "We have rules and stipulations to discuss. And you're about to be very happy you brought comfortable chairs, because this could take all night." ⌒

Davis

*F*IVE MONTHS LATER...

Davis Cain glowered at the gas gauge, as if he could intimidate it into fluttering, at least far enough above empty to get him home. Naturally, it didn't budge.

You've got to work on that glower, he imagined his cousin, Curtis, taunting with a laugh. *It doesn't even scare rabbits.*

Davis got out of the car and slammed the door. If this wasn't the fucking capper on a fucking shitty night. He opened the door and slammed it again, for added effect. Not that there was anyone around to hear it. Not on this dirt road, without a house in sight.

Of course there wasn't a fucking house in sight, because that would be too easy. Why the hell did his uncle need to live out here anyway?

Because he was a werewolf. Because they all were—Davis and his uncle Lonny and Curtis. It made sense to live out here, where they could run and hunt in peace and safety.

That was the logical explanation. Davis did not want logical explanations. He wanted to be at his uncle's place now, stepping out of a car that had enough goddamned gas to get him there.

Except, once he did get there, he'd have to listen to Curtis razz him about being home so early from his date.

Should have taken me up on my offer, Curtis would say. *I've told you before, I can fix you up with a guaranteed score.*

But Davis didn't want a guaranteed score. He didn't want a score at all...well, okay, that would've been nice, but all he'd really wanted was a good first date. A chance to make an impression on a girl he really liked. A girl who'd spent the entire meal checking her phone.

He'd told himself maybe she was expecting an important call. Which she was, apparently, and it came right when they'd been walking to the movie. A call from her recent ex. Who was really, really sorry and if she'd just talk to him, maybe come by, and grab a drink at the bar where he worked? Soon? Like, tonight?

Oh, Davis, I'm so sorry to cut tonight short. Dinner was great, but my friend, she's sick and she really needs me to come over.

Sick friend? Seriously? He'd had to accept the excuse and smile, not letting on that his werewolf hearing had picked up both sides of the phone conversation.

It was, Davis had to admit, his own damned fault. He knew she'd just broken up with the guy last week. He'd leapt in, hoping to woo her away before her ex could try winning her back. A risky gamble. One Davis had known he'd probably lose, but he had to try anyway, because he liked her. Damn it, he really liked her. And now she hadn't just ditched him— she'd proven she wasn't the kind of girl he thought she was.

Davis checked the trunk for a gas can. He knew there wouldn't be one—that would require foresight on his uncle's part. But he checked anyway and still slammed the trunk when he found it empty. Then he kicked the tire, just because, and that was fucking stupid, leaving him dancing around on one foot, having forgotten he was wearing dress shoes instead of his usual steel-toed boots.

Fuck it, fuck it, fuck!

That didn't really help either. He'd been injecting more profanity into his language since coming to live with his uncle last year. Toned down the college-boy diction, too, because, well, he wasn't a college boy anymore, was he? He'd just started his sophomore year when he got his first Change. It might have taken its sweet time, but when it came, it hit with a vengeance. He'd struggled to control the timing but there was only so much he could do. He'd barely made it to the nearest patch of forest, which was also where kids were hanging out, partying.

He hadn't hurt anyone. But he'd been spotted, and it hit the local paper—Big Wolf on Campus, ha-ha. His great-uncle Theo heard about it and hauled Davis's ass back home before the Pack noticed the article and eliminated the problem. Because that's what the Pack did—one screw-up and you're dead.

Or that's what Uncle Theo said, and since he was the Cain clan patriarch, Davis listened to him, even if...well, even if Uncle Theo wasn't the brightest bulb. Theo was, however, the brightest elder in the clan, which was, yeah, kinda sad, but Davis always felt disloyal thinking that, so he reminded himself that they were family and they were good to him. They just weren't always *right* about stuff. Including the Pack.

At Christmas, Davis had gone to New York State on a dare. Really stupid, considering it was Pack territory, but with his late Change and his year of college and the fact he'd lost the only two challenges he'd ever fought... His cousins razzed him. A lot. They'd all been drinking and Carter dared him to go up to Pack territory and get a picture of the Pack's estate—Stonehaven—to prove he'd been there. Davis had been drunk enough to say yes...and proud enough not to change his mind when he sobered up.

He'd gone to Stonehaven and had been trying to figure out how to get a photo of the house without setting foot on the property when he bumped into one of the Alpha's kids. The boy, who wasn't more than eight or nine and smelled like he was already a full werewolf, which wasn't possible. Anyway, the kid's dad came by, and the kid's dad was Clayton Danvers, the psycho his father used to threaten him with when he was little. *Do what you're told, boy, or I'll take you up to Stonehaven and drop you off on their front porch. You know what Clayton Danvers does to trespassers? Cuts them up with a chainsaw. While they're still alive.*

Obviously Clayton had not cut Davis up. He'd gotten Davis's story and rolled his eyes and called him an idiot. A dumb kid making a really dumb life choice, one that could have *ended* his life. Clayton made sure Davis hadn't actually set foot on the property—and hadn't touched his kid—and then he let him off with a warning. He'd even given him some advice for fighting challenges: hit the books and wise up. Which was ironic, considering that Davis wanted nothing more than to hit the books, go back to college and finish his degree. That wasn't happening, though. Not anytime soon. *Cains don't need no stinkin' education.* He'd been lucky Uncle Theo let him go to high school—other Cains were home-schooled.

As for Clayton Danvers, Davis hadn't told anyone he'd met him and lived to tell the tale. If a guy gives you a second chance, you don't kick him in the ass for it.

Still, he couldn't blame Uncle Theo for hating the Pack. They'd killed his son, Zack, about fifteen years ago. And they'd messed up his youngest, Ford, leaving him with a missing ear and a whole lotta scars.

Right now, Davis's problems were far more mundane: a shitty date and his own stupidity in not filling the gas tank. And the stupid car, running out of gas.

Sure, Uncle Lonny had said. *Take my car for your hot date, Davey-boy. Just remember to fill 'er up in town. She'll be running on fumes by the time you get there.*

Davis had been heading to the gas station when he'd passed a florist and decided to buy flowers. Then he didn't have time to stop for gas. Afterwards, he'd been so upset about getting ditched that he'd totally forgotten to fill up. Which left him with time to reflect and ruminate on werewolf politics, given that he had a five-mile walk back to Uncle Lonny's.

He was less than a hundred feet from the driveway when he realized his uncle's house was silent. That wasn't possible, not when his uncle and cousin were both home. It was almost midnight on a Saturday. Time for both to be roaring drunk, TV blaring, and enjoying the fact they were too far from the neighbors to deal with noise complaints.

They hadn't gone out for the evening. He could see Curtis's truck in the lane, beside his rusting Honda. Had they

Changed and gone running? Highly unlikely. They'd done that just a few days ago, the three of them.

He reached the driveway and peered up at the small rented house. It was totally dark, without even the bluish glow of the big-screen TV lighting up the windows. Of course, if the TV was on, he'd have heard it before he got this far. His uncle and cousin might have werewolves' sensitive hearing, but everything they did was loud, from talking to moving to watching TV. Hell, they even snored at a hundred decibels.

Every cell in his body said that silence spelled trouble. Big trouble. The problem was... Well, Davis remembered hearing his clan talking about him last summer, after he failed the second challenge they'd arranged.

When God was giving out brains, Davey-boy got himself in line twice. Problem is, he was so busy making sure he was smart that he missed the line for backbone.

You think too much, Davey, Uncle Theo would say. *That's why you can't win a challenge. You're thinking while they're swinging.*

True. He could fight, but when it came to werewolf challenges, he just couldn't stop thinking, "What's the point?" To earn a rep. He knew that. But they were werewolves, not professional boxers. They had to know how to survive. And maybe part of that was fighting, but just because a guy could take on all comers in a fair bout didn't mean he'd survive in the real world.

Stop thinking. Start doing.

Davis growled under his breath, his family's influence warring against the part that didn't give a shit if he was caught creeping in the back door, jumping at shadows while Curtis laughed at his cowardly little cousin, because caution was the better part of valor. Or something like that.

So he did what he usually did. Embraced his cautious side. He backed up and crept through the forest around the house. The woods started less than ten paces from the door, which was one reason his uncle rented this place. Even in West Virginia, winter nights got cold. Best if you could Change inside, prop the door open and make a run for it. It wasn't like there were neighbors around to see you.

Davis stopped to sniff the rear steps. Obvious, right? Not for other Cains. They'd ask what he was going to do if he *did* scent an intruder. Run? Well, no—he'd be forewarned. But they didn't understand that, even when Davis tried to explain it. To them caution equaled cowardice. Better to just barrel on in, confident you could handle whatever might lurk within.

He picked up only the scents of his uncle and cousin and himself. Very recent for Uncle Lonny and Curtis, suggesting they *had* gone out back. Maybe got drunk enough that they forgot the pain of the Change and said, "Why not?" It was a good night for a run. Warm and clear with a full moon.

That full moon didn't force a werewolf to Change, but it was a bonus, the extra light boosting their night vision.

Davis climbed the steps. The back door was open. Not just unlocked, but cracked open.

He went inside and listened. The house was silent and dark.

Okay, so they must have left. And actually remembered to turn everything off first—as he reminded them so often that they'd begun calling him Mr. Greenpeace, which, yeah, pretty much summed up their knowledge of conservation. They got better at it after he pointed out the difference in their electrical bill.

As Davis headed from the back room into the kitchen, he stumbled over his cousin's size twelve work boots.

"Damn it, Curtis, we're going to kill ourselves tripping over those. Put them in the closet."

"But I'd have to get them out every time I want to leave."

Grumbling, Davis picked up the boots. Sometimes he felt like the adult with both his uncle and thirty-year-old cousin.

He was setting the boots on the mat when he stopped. Uncle Lonny's boots were there, toppled over as usual. As were Davis's, neatly straightened at the side. But if their boots were here...

His uncle and cousin didn't own other footwear. They didn't see the point. Davis had even once watched Curtis dress for a date in Davis's "job interview" suit jacket and tie with jeans and work boots.

"Hey, she's a classy chick. I can't go looking like a slob."

Curtis's boots. Uncle Lonny's boots. Inside.

If they Changed form before going out, there'd be discarded clothing on every kitchen surface. Even in the near dark, Davis could see only the usual soda bottles and beer cans and takeout cartons, all accumulated since he'd tidied up this morning.

God, I want to go back to college. Give me the worst roommate ever. I'm ready for him.

He walked into the kitchen and looked through to the TV room. No sign of them. Bedrooms? Bathroom? Nothing.

At the front door, he dropped and sniffed. Again, it was just his family.

He stood in the kitchen, arms crossed.

Okay, Sherlock. Figure it out.

It was a prank. Had to be. Let's give college boy's brain a workout. Except to come up with a prank that would stump Davis they'd actually need to think up one and... Yeah. *Sorry, guys, I love you, but that's not happening.* Not when, as the "smart one" in the family, he'd still barely squeaked into college, aided by a football scholarship.

He missed football. Fuck, how he missed it. Football, college, college pubs, college towns, college girls...

Stop feeling sorry for yourself and solve the mystery.

He did another circuit of the house. Even checked under the beds, as if his six-foot-four, two-hundred-and-fifty-pound uncle or cousin would fit under one. Hell, Davis was two inches shorter and fifty pounds lighter and *he* hadn't been able to hide from his father under a bed since he was twelve.

Finally, he opened the front door, ready to shout for his uncle and brother to come out, come out, wherever they were. That's when he smelled it. The fresh scent of strangers on their porch.

He backed up fast and closed the door.

Um, Davey…?

He ignored the little mental voice that called his bravery into question, went into the front room and peered through the half-drawn blinds. Then he returned to the door, opened it and carefully scanned the darkness. He dropped to all fours. Three separate scents. No, four. Shit, no—five. Five men on their porch. One of them…a werewolf? He thought he picked up that musky scent, but it was hard to tell with all the other scents, including those of the three werewolves who lived here.

But there had definitely been five strangers on their porch, and the chances that any of them had been canvassing for cancer research was less than zero. In the year he'd been here, only one person had knocked on their door— a neighbor's kid selling Girl Scout cookies and knowing the Cains were fine customers when it came to consumables.

This was no Girl Scout troop.

He paced back and forth on the porch, committing the scents to memory as his brain kept looping through the question, "Why would Uncle Lonny and Curtis run?" Even against five men, he could not imagine them fleeing.

But they had. And the men *had* pursued—they just hadn't gone through the house. Davis followed the strangers' trail around the side and into the woods. Then he found his uncle and cousin's recent trail crossing it.

A straight trail.

A trail of panic. Two big men, knocking down everything in their path, like grizzlies charging through the forest.

Then he realized it wasn't panic. It was determination—the kind of thinking that ran in an equally straight line from thought to execution, from plan to goal. That goal became apparent when the trail led to the thicket they used for Changing. Inside, he found their clothing, yanked off and thrown aside, with paw prints in damp ground leading out.

Davis was stepping from that thicket himself when he caught the acrid smell of gunpowder. That's when he understood.

Five men. Armed with guns. At the front door. That was a fight his uncle and cousin couldn't win. Slam the door. Run out the back. No time for footwear when it'd come off in a few minutes. Hightail it to the thicket. Get inside. Change forms.

And the hunted becomes the hunter. Circle back and start picking off your prey.

It was not the best plan. But it was a shrewd one.

Davis listened. The forest was eerily silent. He glanced at the scattered clothing and considered Changing to help. But if there was a fight in progress, wouldn't he hear it?

Not if his uncle and cousin were still stalking their prey. Or if they'd driven them deeper into the forest.

As he walked a few more steps, he heard a branch creak in the wind. He tried to pick up a more distant sound—a grunt or a growl. But once he heard the damned branch, it was all he could hear. That constant *creak-creak*. Pause. *Creak-creak*.

Davis rolled his shoulders. Ignore that and find his uncle and cousin. He wouldn't Change. Not yet.

With every step, he swore that damned branch got louder. *Creak-creak*. Pause. *Creak-creak*.

He finally gave up and headed in that direction. At least it gave him a point of reference.

He was almost there when the wind changed direction, making the branch give a triple creak...and blowing a scent into his face. The coppery smell of blood.

He rubbed his hand over his nose. At least that much blood meant he wasn't smelling the result of a gun wound. This was violent death, by ripping fangs and powerful jaws.

His uncle and cousin hadn't just broken a few necks. They'd separated a couple of men from the group and torn them to shreds so when the others stumbled over the bodies, they'd get the message: Don't screw with the Cains.

He took a few more steps, still following that creaking branch. The blood-laden wind blew straight in his face. Shit, that was bad. Blood and shit and piss and every other stench that accompanied violent death. Enough to make his stomach churn. He put his hand over his nose and took another step and…

His gaze rose…

"Fuck."

He said the word before he could stop himself, and then looked around quickly. But there was no one here. No one except…

Fuck.

His uncle and cousin hadn't settled for slaughtering a couple of their pursuers and leaving the bodies for the others to find. They'd strung one up. That's what he'd heard—a body hanging from a tree, making the branch creak in protest.

It was heavily wooded here, the moon passing behind clouds. He could just make out the shape of the corpse. Long and lean. Weirdly shaped. And…naked? The figure was pale against the darkness. Definitely stripped naked. With something behind it.

With another body behind it. He saw that as he continued forward. Two tall and lean men, stripped and strung up by their arms. But the shapes were just...weird. What the hell was...

The cloud cover passed and the moon shone down, filtering through the trees, illuminating the bodies, and he saw it wasn't two men. It was two giant wolves, hanging by their forepaws.

Two skinned wolves. ⌒

One

I'D BEEN FIVE months since I met Malcolm in Bulgaria. Five months since I sat in that clearing and laid out the list of rules and stipulations Jeremy and Clay and I had spent over a month hammering through.

We'd given Malcolm territory. Not in Bulgaria, as tempting as that might be. Pack territory is New York State. One member, Karl, lives outside it, in Philadelphia. So we gave Malcolm Pittsburgh. He wasn't happy. But as long as he wasn't living on our doorstep, *we* were happy and that's what mattered.

Malcolm was not permitted on our doorstep. He was not permitted on our territory without express permission. If we so much as caught him taking in a Broadway show, the deal was off. He would be allowed in for Pack Meets. The first one after his readmittance, though, had been Thanksgiving, followed by Christmas, and he sure as hell wasn't coming to Stonehaven for the holidays. The next one should have been in February, but we went skiing in Vermont instead, and since that was more of a social get-together, there was no reason for him to come. Then came Easter and—

"You can't keep doing this," Jeremy said.

"Yep, pretty sure I can."

He gave me a hard look. "You cannot have a Pack wolf who doesn't attend Pack Meets."

"We haven't had real Pack Meets since he joined."

"You're exploiting a loophole."

"That's what loopholes are for."

Another look, and this one wasn't hard, it was just endless, as I struggled not to squirm like a student caught cheating on her exam.

"I will be fine," he said finally.

"Of course you will. That's not why—"

"Yes, it is. You don't want him in the Pack, but you particularly don't want him coming here. To Stonehaven."

"It's not—"

"I spent thirty years exhaling every time he walked out that door. Dreading every time he came back. And then another decade jumping each time I heard the knob turn, expecting he wasn't really dead." He caught my gaze. "I haven't done that in twenty years. Not since the day I heard that knob turn and thought I heard his voice, and I *didn't* jump. I realized then that I didn't care if he came back because I wasn't a child anymore. I was the Alpha. I *felt* like the Alpha. That took a long time, as I'm sure you know. When I finally felt like the Alpha, it became my defining role. Not Malcolm Danvers' son. The American Alpha."

He lowered his voice. "I know what you're thinking, Elena. I know why you hate this so much. To you, it's as if I'd let one of the men from your childhood into the Pack. But it *isn't* like that. I beat Malcolm when I won the Alpha race. And I've kept beating him, in every way. He's been held captive, forced to work for the Nasts, then on the run, never having a place to rest, never able to rest. What kind of a life is that? I have a house—his house. I have a family—Clayton, you and the twins. I have Jaime. I have a flourishing career. And I'm rich." His lips twitched. "The last hardly registers on my list, but I know it would be near the top of his."

When I still didn't reply, he said, "Let him come, Elena. I have nothing to hide. Nothing I am ashamed of. I have won, in every possible way, and while I'd like to say it won't please me for him to see that..." He met my gaze. "If there's part of me that is still the little boy who quaked at the sound of his voice, it will be very gratified to see him come here as a guest in my home, as a wolf in your Pack. As the *omega* wolf in your Pack."

I exhaled. "All right. After Easter, I'll—"

"No, Elena. You're going to call a Meet now and get this over with. For all of us."

I scheduled the Meet. I didn't find some excuse to cancel it, or some reason why Malcolm couldn't attend, though I may have had to fight—hard—against the impulse. I wasn't the only one, either.

"Antonio says we could move it to their place," Clay said, two days before the Meet. "Their estate *is* bigger. And so is the Pack. We have eleven adult members now. Twelve if you include him. Plus Jaime, Vanessa, Hope and four kids... It only makes sense to start holding full Meets at the Sorrentino estate."

Jeremy kiboshed the suggestion with nothing more than a look.

Then came the night before the big day, when Malcolm phoned for last-minute arrangements, and I said, "The Meet is at ten Saturday morning. It will last until late afternoon."

"I thought it lasted all weekend."

"That's the social part."

"In the old days, everyone attended the social part."

"Everyone still does. Except you." I lowered my voice, a warning growl slipping in. "You know the rules. Don't complain about them now. You are in the Pack for protection and *as* protection. We watch out for you, and you will do any

Pack-related tasks I assign. That means you come for Meet business and nothing more. Now, as I was saying, it starts at ten. You will not show up one minute sooner. Hope and Vanessa will have the kids gone by nine-thirty—"

"So I don't get to meet your children before the Meet?"

"You don't get to meet my children at all. Or Karl's."

"Well, I'm not nearly as interested in his." A moment of silence. "Though he did just have a boy, didn't he? And the mother is Lucifer's daughter. A werewolf with chaos demon blood. That does pique my interest."

"You are not taking an interest in any of our children," I said through clenched teeth.

"That may have been an unfortunate word choice. But part of my job is to protect them, is it not?"

"Only insomuch as all the Pack protects all Pack members."

"Mmm, no. I believe—"

"I'm sure as hell not appointing you as bodyguard to my children. Or Karl's."

"Not literally their bodyguard. Unless we reach the point where you trust me to do that, which I hope we will. They should meet me, though. I'm a Pack member now. They are Pack. At least three of them. Karl's daughter—"

"—is Pack. All our children are."

"That's an...interesting way to handle it. I suppose, though, being a woman, you're more sensitive to her plight."

"Can't even make it to your first Meet without snarking about a female Alpha, can you?"

"I don't believe I was *snarking,* as you put it. I was making an observation devoid of judgment. It's unfortunate about the girl child. At least yours doesn't have that deficiency. A hereditary full-blooded female werewolf, Changing forms before her tenth birthday. I am very interested to meet... That is to say, I'm eager— No, that's probably worse. I would *like* to meet your daughter. And your son, of course. You may want to hide your children from the big, bad wolf, but I would argue you do them a disservice in that."

"Then I do them a disservice. Ten a.m. Be here. Or don't."

When I hung up, I didn't even need to look at Jeremy. I could feel his gaze on me and my, "What?" may have held a bit of a snap.

"He's right," he said. "You do Kate and Logan a disservice if you don't let them meet him."

"A disservice? Not introducing them to that psycho? I don't trust—"

"Which is exactly why they need to meet him," Jeremy said softly.

I glanced at Clay, sitting with me on the sofa. His eyes narrowed, and he crossed his arms. Then he uncrossed them, as if realizing how that made him look—like the boy who'd once sat on this couch and listened to Jeremy tell him he really had to go to school.

"He has a point."

That *was* a little boy's voice. Logan peeked around the doorway, as if checking to see whether furniture was flying before he ventured in. Jeremy waved him in.

I looked at my son. Nine years old. Already a full werewolf, but still small for his age, like his father had been. My silver-blond hair. Clay's bright blue eyes. The perfect blend of both parents, with a look on his face that made him seem much older—or at least much more mature—than either.

"Jeremy has a point, Mom. We want to meet Malcolm—"

A snort from the doorway. Kate walked through, arms crossed almost exactly like her father's, and the scowl on her face probably an exact mirror of my own a moment ago. A five-month-old black and white puppy tumbled along at her heels. Atalanta parked herself between them and straightened, as if sensing the seriousness of the conversation.

"No," Kate said. "We don't *want* to meet Malcolm. He's a murdering psychopathic son of a—"

"Kate," I said.

"Son of a beyotch."

"That's not really better."

"It's true, though. We know what Malcolm is. We've had werewolf hearing since we were babies, remember? You might send us away for Meets—which, personally, I also think does us a disservice—but we hear enough to know what Malcolm is. Which is exactly why we need to meet him. Look him in the eye and let him know if he so much as touches us, he'll regret it."

"I think *regret* might be pushing it," Logan said.

"I don't."

Atalanta growled, as if in agreement.

"The point," Logan said, "is that by meeting him, we put a face and a scent to his name, and he knows it. He will also see that we are *not* intrigued by him. Nor are we afraid of him. Which isn't to say we don't know exactly how dangerous he is, but he doesn't scare us."

He should, baby. That's what I wanted to say, and yet Logan was right, in his oh-so-logical way. There might not be a blood connection between him and Jeremy, but I see so much of Jeremy in him.

"We'll ask Ness to bring us back for lunch," Logan said.

"I don't think Vanessa—"

"Or Jaime. Or Hope, if she's okay leaving the baby. Someone will bring us back and we'll have lunch with him, and then we'll leave." ⌒

Two

MEET DAY.

Everyone had arrived the night before. As Clay said, the Pack was getting big for Stonehaven, but we hadn't outgrown it yet. Karl and Hope stayed at a hotel in Syracuse, which was easier with the baby. Our kids gave up their rooms to sleep in the study with Atalanta. Everyone else just found a bed or a couch or other suitable horizontal surface and made do.

At nine, we bundled the kids off with Hope. Jaime was meeting up with them later. Vanessa had been delayed by unexpected business in New York City. Karl had gone with Hope until Jaime could join them—looking after a two-month-old baby, a toddler and two werewolf children was a little much, even for a chaos half-demon.

At nine-thirty, Malcolm called from Bear Valley to say he was running ahead of schedule. Did I want him to wait in town? I couldn't tell if he was making the effort to follow directions or being an ass. I told him it was fine, just come over.

Jeremy was in the driveway, seeing Jaime off, when Malcolm arrived, and I realized that she hadn't lingered because she'd wanted to sleep in. She'd dawdled to be there, with Jeremy, when Malcolm arrived. I was still out the door the moment I heard a car in the drive...and I was already three paces behind Clay.

When Malcolm pulled up, the four of us were in the drive, waiting.

"A welcoming committee," he said as he got out. "Or am I to be frisked before I cross the threshold?"

"They were seeing me off," Jaime said. She kissed Jeremy's cheek and murmured, "I'll come back at lunch with the kids." Then, without waiting for an introduction, she headed for her car.

"That must be the famous Jaime Vegas, celebrity spiritualist and necromancer," Malcolm said as he watched her go. "I would say she looks better on television, but I really can't." He tilted his head as she went, his gaze glued to Jaime's ass. "No, I really can't."

"Enough," I said.

He looked over at me, blue eyes widening. "I was complimenting—"

"I warned you not to insult the mates of any Pack wolf. That includes ogling and leering."

"I don't see how that's an insult."

"Believe me, it is."

"Hello, Malcolm," Jeremy said.

"Oh, you're going to acknowledge me?"

"I was letting Elena finish."

"Always so polite."

Malcolm turned toward Jeremy for the first time since he'd arrived. Even when he'd spoken to him, he hadn't actually looked over. Now he did, and I held my breath. Clay rocked forward, as if just waiting for an excuse.

Jeremy had not seen his father since the day he won the Alphahood. Now, as he turned his gaze on him, I remembered when I first joined the Pack. At the time, Jeremy had seemed not my savior but my captor. What I'd hated most was his unassailable poker face. I could cry and rant and threaten, and I'd get no reaction. Even later I hated that face. I felt like the little girl, desperate to please her father and so rarely even coaxing a smile. But that was Jeremy, and I'd learned to read the tiny signs that hinted at his mood. Now, as he looked at his father, I couldn't even pick up those, and I was glad of it, so damned glad of it, because it meant Malcolm got nothing. Thirty years and he didn't even get the satisfaction of a reaction.

"Let's go in," I said, and started toward the house, Clay on one side, Jeremy on the other. Which meant Malcolm had to follow along, like the omega he now was. It also meant we had our backs to him. That was a message too, the same one my son wanted to give—that we were not afraid.

"The twins are coming back for lunch," I said. "You'll meet them then."

"Changed your mind?"

I ignored the smugness in his voice. If I'd stuck to my decision he'd have gloated over *that*, as a sign of fear. There would be no winning with Malcolm. I would have to just refuse to play his game. Starting with not tensing and growling every time he smirked and snarked. That's how he wins.

"Everyone will be at this Meet except Charlie Gray," I said. "He had business back home, so I gave him a pass."

"Flights don't run on Saturdays?"

"He's in Australia."

"I thought the Australian pup wasn't allowed to set foot back home."

"That's Reese. We have three Australians."

"What's wrong with American werewolves? Or is the question, What's wrong with the Pack that makes it unattractive to American werewolves?"

"Seemed attractive enough to you," Clay said as he opened the front door. "If you want another option, though, I'd suggest the Australians. Bunch of fucking thugs. You'd fit right in." He looked at Malcolm as he held the door. "And, yeah, Elena and Jeremy will rise above the insult-banter, but I'm not as mature as them. You know what I'll find even more fun, though?" He leaned over as Malcolm walked through. "When you break one of Elena's rules. If you could hurry it up, I'd appreciate that."

"Oh, he won't break any rules today," I said. "He'll just tread along the boundary. Like a kid sticking his toe over the safe line. *Nyah-nyah-nyah, you can't get me.*"

Clay snorted a laugh. Even Jeremy's lips twitched. I don't know what Malcolm did. I didn't bother to look.

We headed into the front hall, me saying, "Antonio, Nick and Morgan are in the study. Karl's on his way. I'm not sure where—"

The back door banged open, and Atalanta's frenzied barking echoed through the house, along with the pound of half-a-dozen feet.

"Come on, girl," Reese said. "Jump for it. Jump!"

"Don't give her a muffin," Madison said. "You'll make her sick."

"Oh, I didn't mean the dog. Come on, Maddie. Jump for the muffin! You can— *Oomph.*"

Then, "Hey! Noah!" from Madison. A bark from Atalanta. A yelp from Noah, along with, "Not my fingers, pup!" and the dog tore past with a muffin in her mouth.

"Are you sure we sent all the kids off with Hope and Karl this morning?" Clay asked.

Reese, Maddie and Noah came tumbling around the corner, not unlike a pack of puppies themselves, bickering and smacking each other. They saw me and stopped.

"No horsing around in the house, guys." Maddie said as she rolled her eyes at me. "Boys. Also? In case you didn't figure it out yet, Reese is an asshole."

"Excuse me?" Reese said. "I baked muffins this morning, just for you."

"No, you made muffins for everyone. You only saved one for me and let the dog get it."

"Noah let the dog—"

"I grabbed it for Maddie," Noah cut in.

"Guys?" I said. "Cool it. Reese made two batches of muffins, Maddie. He's just giving you a hard time. If you can put the rest on a tray and bring them into the living room, I'd appreciate that. Boys? Coffee duty."

Malcolm cleared his throat. He was still partly around the corner, and they obviously hadn't seen him there. Madison looked first. She sized him up, nodded curtly and started past him.

I still wanted to introduce them without everyone else hanging around. Karl was supposed to call me from outside. Instead, he'd walked in, and before I could run interference, he was already passing us with a, "Hello, Malcolm" before continuing on, deep in conversation with Noah, leaving Malcolm staring after him.

Malcolm shut up once the Meet started. He was, at heart, still a Pack wolf. And a Pack wolf knows that once we get down to business, you shut up and listen.

Some Pack business is internal—a rundown of who's doing what and how it affects their responsibilities. Like Noah having to move a planned training trip with Karl due to changes in his college mid-term schedule. Most business is external—what's going on in the wider werewolf world.

Madison and Reese had taken over my old job of scouring the Internet for news of potential werewolf trouble. They'd found reports of a wild canine kill in Alberta, but it seemed to be a wolf-dog, locals filling the comment section with stories about a guy who'd had trouble with his hybrid and released it into the wild. Reese had checked with Nick—who's in charge of the dossiers these days—and they hadn't found any reports of mutts in that area of Alberta. We'd keep an eye on the news, but I wouldn't send anyone to investigate.

As for Nick's dossier work, he and Vanessa had been tracking the movements of a mutt who'd emigrated from

Three

KARL'S ARRIVAL PRESENTED yet another problem, one I was as unsuccessful at avoiding as I'd been with Jeremy. I wanted to protect everyone from Malcolm. And they refused to be protected. Which was damned annoying.

Karl had been fifteen when Malcolm murdered his father, leaving Karl to fend for himself after narrowly escaping the same fate. Yet Hope said he felt almost the same way as Jeremy—that Karl didn't really give a shit about Malcolm anymore. Like Jeremy, he'd overcome any impact Malcolm had on his life. He had a reputation that rivaled Malcolm's, a wife, two children and a massive bank account from a successful career. Okay, it was a career as a jewel thief, but Malcolm was hardly the sort to find fault with that.

just a friend—albeit a very good one. That growl when he warned off Malcolm suggested there might be more growing there. I just hoped he did something about it before she gave up and found someone else.

The doorbell rang as I introduced Reese and Noah.

"That'd be Karl," Noah said. "I'll get it."

"Ah, yes. Karl Marsten," Malcolm said. "The mutt who joined a rebellion to take down the Pack. Was Pack membership his reward for failing? Or for betraying his fellow mutts? Because *that's* the kind of werewolf you want in the Pack. A rebel and a traitor."

I shook my head and started for the front door. This was going to be the longest Meet ever. ⌐⌐

"I thought all the girlfriends had left for the Meet."

"I'm not a girlfriend," she said. "I'm Pack."

"Madison is Charlie's daughter." I resisted the urge to say that she grew up with her father and understood werewolf culture. That she came with valuable skills—her dad is a PI and trained her. That she pulled her weight as much as Reese and Noah. All that sounds like I'm defending a decision I don't need to defend. Not to him.

Instead I said, "She's a full Pack member."

"Really? That's a…unique approach to recruitment."

"I know," she said. "They just let anyone in these days, don't they?" A pointed look at him, and she continued into the kitchen.

Malcolm watched her go, much the same way he'd watched Jaime.

"She's young enough to be your *great*-granddaughter." Reese said with a growl.

"Doesn't mean I can't appreciate the view. I'm guessing she's yours?"

"She's my friend."

"Ouch. What's the term kids use? Friend-zoned?"

"No one uses that term," Noah said. "Except old guys trying to look cool."

Reese's parents had died because he'd fallen for the wrong girl. A girl who'd been a werewolf's daughter. So Madison was

49

Albania six months ago. Nick lost track of him a few weeks ago. I decided this one did deserve a little more attention—the mutt's movements were erratic, with lots of cross-country flights. Nick would fly to the mutt's last known location next week and do some legwork.

We were discussing that when Atalanta leaped up from her position at my side and tore off with a happy bark. A moment later the front door opened and Kate trilled, "We're home!"

I glanced around the room. As if I'd transmitted a message by mental telepathy, Nick, Antonio, Karl, Morgan and Noah all rose, Antonio saying, "We'll be in the yard. Shout when lunch is ready."

"I'll join them," Jeremy said, and he shot me a quick look to say this was better—just Clay and me with the kids. I nodded and went to the front door to collect them. ⌒

Four

KATE MARCHED IN ahead of me, Atalanta at her heels. She stopped in front of Malcolm and looked him up and down.

"So you're Malcolm."

"I am," he said.

She snorted and—just in case he missed that sign of exactly how unimpressed she was—she added an eye roll. Our girl is not subtle.

Kate turned to Clay and me. "I thought you said he didn't look old."

Malcolm choked on a laugh. "Oh, you are your father's daughter. You must be Katie."

"It's Kate."

A slight twitch of his lips. Atalanta growled, and Malcom smiled at the dog.

"And what's your pup's name?"

"Atalanta," Kate said.

"After the city?"

"At-a-lanta," Kate said. "From Greek mythology. She was a huntress who would only marry a man who beat her in a foot race. She was fast and a good hunter, just like *our* Atalanta."

Malcolm looked confused. He shook it off and leaned to the side, just now catching a glimpse of Logan. "Hiding behind your sister, boy?"

"No." Logan stepped up beside her. "I was being polite and waiting my turn."

"Polite." Malcolm rolled the word around, and as his gaze traveled over Logan, I realized I was holding my breath. The expression on Malcolm's face was exactly what I feared. He looked at Kate and saw Clay. He looked at Logan…and he did not see Clay or me.

Oh, there's lots of us both there. Logan has my intensity and, unfortunately, my tendency to overthink things and worry too much. There's just as much of his father. Most people see only Clay's snarl and growl, but he has a quiet side, a deep intellectual side—the part I'm sure Malcolm had tried to overlook and blame on Jeremy's influence.

Everyone says Malcolm hated Jeremy because he isn't a rough and tumble wolf. That's partly true. It's more true to

say that Malcolm doesn't understand him. And what Malcolm doesn't understand makes him uncomfortable, even fearful.

Jeremy is not a typical werewolf and yet Jeremy is successful as a werewolf. Malcolm cannot resolve that seeming contradiction. He sees his son's quiet nature, his unfailing politeness, his quiet and even temper and thinks, *That's unnatural.*

And now, he looked at our son and saw the same thing, and I wanted to snatch Logan back, to spit and snarl at Malcolm and send him away before he did anything, *anything*, to make my son feel different.

Yet my eerily brilliant, eerily focused, eerily mature son *is* different, and he knows it—no school-age child can avoid that. But he doesn't care, no more than his sister cares about her quirks.

The Pack accepts Logan's uniqueness, as they do Kate's and Clay's and everyone's. They are simply variations in personality that make us special. Jeremy had a more difficult time growing up—some in the Pack are like true wolves, uncomfortable with non-conformity, driven to root it out. Logan doesn't need to endure that so he is, in his way, as confident as his sister. The regard of one man—particularly a man who his Pack despises—will not shake that confidence. I must remember that.

"Reese, Maddie and Noah are out back," I said, "if you two want to—"

"We're fine." Kate plunked down on the sofa, her gaze fixed on Malcolm in a way that made Clay smile.

We all took seats. And we sat there, in silence, until Logan said to Malcolm, "Did you learn much Bulgarian while you were there?"

"What?" Malcolm said.

"Bulgarian," Kate said. "It's the language they speak in Bulgaria, where you lived for the last couple of years. Logan is asking if you bothered to learn any."

Malcolm stared at them as if trying to ferret out some subtext in the question.

"I know a little," Logan said. "I can speak more Russian, but Bulgarian has lexical similarities."

"They're both Cyrillic languages," Kate said.

"Yes, but it's more a matter of history," Logan said. "At one time, Russian was taught in Bulgarian schools. Now more students learn English than Russian, so Malcolm wouldn't have had too difficult a time there. I'm sure he still picked up some. I considered greeting him with Здравейте, как сте but..."

"That would be showing off," Kate said.

"Which is why I didn't."

Kate turned to Malcolm. "Logan likes languages."

Logan shrugged and said, "Jeremy teaches me," and I cringed, but Clay chuckled. *That* was no innocent comment, no more than the topic was accidental. My precocious son understood exactly what Malcolm was picking up...and he was needling him.

"Karl actually knows more languages than Jeremy," Kate said.

"True," Logan said. "Karl's been teaching us Japanese. I did a school project on samurais and all the best sources were in Japanese."

"I've been learning it too," Kate said. "So I can read manga in the original."

"Translations are good," Logan said, "but they miss subtleties, especially with humor."

Kate nodded. "I'm learning Japanese. Some French. My Spanish is pretty good, and my Russian's not bad. No Bulgarian, though." She looked up at Malcolm and said, as sweet as could be, "So, *did* you pick up any Bulgarian? Logan could use help with his accent if you did. You're Pack now, and part of being Pack is helping the younger generation."

Malcolm...well, Malcolm stared. That's all he did. As if he'd been plunged into an episode of the *Twilight Zone*, one where nine-year-olds discussed the subtleties of language and learned Japanese to read original texts. And one where, apparently, nine-year-olds could render Malcolm Danvers speechless.

The phone rang, and I swear he exhaled.

It rang again, and he said, "Isn't someone going to get that?"

"No, they won't," Logan said, rising with a sigh. "Don't ask."

As Logan crossed the room to the desk, Clay said, "There's an answering machine. They'll leave a message."

Logan sighed, deeper, once again saddled with being the responsible one in the family. He answered with, "Danvers residence, Logan Danvers speaking."

Malcolm raised his brows and said, "My, he is very polite."

"It's a twin thing," Kate said. "I'm not polite, so he is *exceedingly* so. We need to establish unique identities."

"I...see."

As the person on the other end of the line spoke, Logan's shoulder muscles tensed. His voice dropped a half-octave and I swear there was a hint of a growl in it as he said, "Yes, I remember you."

I jumped up and reached for the phone, but he turned away smoothly, as if he hadn't noticed me. "My father is busy at the moment. If you'd like to leave a number—"

The caller said something a little louder, and I caught a note of panic in a male voice, but Logan had the receiver pressed too tightly to his ear for me to hear more.

"No, I will not interrupt him. He'll return the call in ten minutes...if he decides to return it. Now, the number?"

The caller gave it. Logan jotted it down and then hung up without a goodbye.

"Well, *that* wasn't polite at all," Kate said. "Some guy's freaking out on the phone and you're making him wait? Dad's sitting right there."

"It's a mutt." Logan tore off the page and handed it to Clay. "We can't jump when they call, even if it does seem urgent." He looked at his father. "It was Davis Cain."

"Davis...?" I stopped. "Oh."

"Yes, the one who tried to take a picture of the house, right before Christmas."

"Tried to take a picture of the house?" Malcolm said.

Logan turned to him. "It was a dare. I caught him walking down one of the side-roads. Dad sent him running."

Malcolm's brows shot up. "There was a mutt on your territory, and he's still alive?"

Clay's jaw tightened, and I cursed Davis Cain's lousy timing. Yes, Clay had let him go. A decision he'd been second-guessing ever since. He really didn't need Malcolm weighing in. I opened my mouth, but Logan beat me to it.

"He was a nineteen-year-old doing something stupid. He didn't set foot on Stonehaven property, and he didn't lay a finger on me."

"Only because he didn't get the chance," Malcolm said. "You caught him and ran for your father?"

Logan's brows shot up. "Running from a threat is foolish and dangerous. And he was on our territory, which means I had to defend it, if only by warning him to get off *before* my father came."

"You stood up to a Cain?"

"Yes. Unfortunately, in keeping with his family's reputation, he lacked the intellect to refuse his cousins' dare." He paused, looking thoughtful. "No, that's not fair. It isn't a matter of intelligence, really. He knew enough not to lay a hand on me, and he realized he'd made a very big mistake. Which also means he's smart enough to realize how close he came to *not* going home."

Malcolm looked at Clay. "You let a mutt walk away—"

"He showed mercy," Kate said. "To a kid bright enough to learn the lesson. You don't kill a teenager for making a stupid mistake."

Logan nodded. "We need to make exceptions to rules for extenuating circumstances. In other situations, a show of force might be necessary, breaking his arm perhaps, but in this case, it would seem like..." He pursed his lips, as if looking for the right word.

"Bullying," Kate said.

"Yes," Logan said. "Davis was terrified, and he'd learned his lesson. More would be bullying."

I cleared my throat. "As much as I'm sure your father loves to hear you two armchair-quarterbacking his decisions..."

DRIVEN

"I see you let your children second-guess their parents," Malcolm said.

"Of course," Logan said. "It allows us to develop critical thinking, which is one trait many werewolves lack. We see their choices and try to understand why they made them."

"In this case, Mom's wording was right," Kate said. "It's armchair-quarterbacking. Not second-guessing. We agree Dad did the right thing."

"Which I appreciate," Clay said. He rolled his eyes for them, but I knew he actually did appreciate that they understood his choice.

"And," I said, "since it was the right decision, there's no more need to remark on it. You two, go out back so we can return this call. Send Antonio in to escort—"

"Malcolm?" Kate said. "Come with us."

I hesitated. To insist on having Antonio do it suggested I feared Malcolm could attack our children under our own roof. I waved for them to go.

Once the back door slammed, Clay sat on the couch, and I took my spot beside him, his arm going around my shoulders.

"The only one second-guessing your decision is you," I said. "Malcolm doesn't count. In fact, I'd go so far as to say if Malcolm thinks you made the wrong choice, then clearly you made the right one."

He chuckled and squeezed my shoulder. But he still didn't say anything. I twisted to face him.

"Two reasons why you're second-guessing," I said. "This—" I tapped the old scarring on his arm. "And the fact that you're getting older. You've spent almost a decade trying to prove that a bad arm doesn't make you any less dangerous than you were before. Now you're wondering if this…" I waved around the room, "…has made you softer. Having kids and a mate. Yes, it has changed you. It means you looked at that Cain boy and you saw Logan in a few years, his friends egging him on to do something stupid."

Clay glanced my way, brows rising.

"All right," I said. "Not Logan but Kate. What if she did something like that as a teenager? You let him go because you've gotten older, wiser, and you see more gray than you used to. It's not the first time we've allowed a Cain to live. Remember the one who stalked me on our honeymoon? We sent him packing. Injured but alive, because he was a dumbass kid following another mutt's lead. You've developed the ability to assess a situation and say, 'The rules don't apply here.'"

"Allow for extenuating circumstances?"

"You've got a smart kid. He takes after his dad."

Clay snorted and then rose. "Yeah, I still feel like I made the right choice—it's just not my natural one. Life's less complicated when you don't see the gray."

"It is. Just ask Malcolm. It's gotten him far. Right back to this living room as omega when he dreamed of being Alpha."

"Looks good on him." He walked to the desk and picked up the paper. "You want to handle this?"

"We'll use my cell and put him on speaker."

"Just block the number first. Bad enough he found our home one."

Five

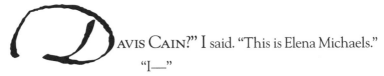AVIS CAIN?" I said. "This is Elena Michaels."

"I—"

"Yes, you called for Clay, but since I'm presuming this is Pack business, you contacted the wrong person. I'm sure that was a mistake. It's an understandable one. In the past, if an outside werewolf wanted to speak to the Alpha, he spoke to his spokesperson instead, which was me. As I'm now Alpha, the procedure has changed. You should contact me directly."

Silence.

"That is why you asked for him, right?" I said. "That plus the fact he's the one you spoke to in December. Not because you believe he's the real Alpha."

"Uh," Davis began. "I've heard that rumor but, uh, I…" A strained laugh. "Typical, huh? Bunch of old guys find out a woman is Alpha, of course they're going to call bullshit." A moment of silence. "So...you really are the Alpha, right?"

Clay closed his eyes and shook his head.

"Yes, I am. Now, Clay is here, listening, as my beta. But unless he asks you a direct question, you'll address me, understood?"

"S-sure."

"So, Logan says you have a problem?"

An odd noise, like a choking, snorting not-quite-laugh. "Yeah, you could say. Oh, fuck. Fuck, fuck, fuck." He stopped. "Sorry. I shouldn't swear. I don't usually. Well, not much but... Shit."

"Davis?" Clay said. "Get to the point. You've called at lunchtime on a Meet day. Everyone's hungry, and no one gets to eat until the Alpha does."

"Right. Sorry. I... I just don't know... I don't even know where to start. It happened last night and I've been on the run since then and... They skinned them. Fuck, they just... Like they were animals. Skinned them and strung them up."

"Skinned who?"

"Lonny and Curtis. My uncle and my cousin."

I mouthed a curse of my own and then said, "Start from the beginning."

THE REST OF the Meet was on hold while I worked this out. I'd sent Karl to Hope and their kids, but I'd told the twins they could stay. They were eating lunch with the others. Jeremy, Clay and I ate in the study, hashing out what Davis had told us.

"So either we have psychos skinning werewolves," Clay said. "Or we're being led into a trap, which the Cains figure we're stupid enough to fall for, after I let their kid go without a scratch."

I looked at him. "You know, there's a point where second-guessing turns into self-flagellation. I think you just crossed it."

His eyes narrowed. "I'm pointing out—"

"That it could be a trap. Excellent. Point that out. Skip the rest."

"Because if you were the one who'd let him go, you wouldn't see it that way?"

"Of course I would. I expect better of you."

He made a face at me.

Jeremy said, "Compared to the Clay who never questions his own actions, this is an improvement. Just don't overdo it."

Clay opened his mouth, but Jeremy cut him off. "Yes, it could turn out to be a trap, possibly precipitated by your decision that night."

"Not helping," I muttered.

"It was a choice. The same one you would have made, Elena. The same one I would have made. The only thing I would have recommended he do differently would have been to call you—the *Alpha*—and get your ruling on it. However, given that I'm sure he spent most of my Alphahood doing things behind my back, rather than put me in the position of making hard choices, I take the blame for that. If he *had* asked you, the only difference now is that you'd be the one second-guessing, and we've had quite enough of that lately over Malcolm."

"Still not helping," Clay said.

"It's a learning experience for all of us. Did Clay's decision help this young werewolf to reach out and alert us to a serious issue? Perhaps. Or did that choice make him think the Pack was weak and easily tricked? If so, then you will show him exactly how wrong he was, and in doing so, you'll prove that we will show mercy but..."

"Woe to those who make us regret it?" I said.

A faint smile. "Exactly. Which is a better message than that imparted by Clay beating a teenage boy."

I stood. "Okay. I'll call Davis and tell him Clay and I are coming. And, of course, we'll bring backup. Nick, Reese and Karl."

Jeremy shook his head. "Karl has a new baby at home. Unless you need his special skills, you should leave him there. He's already helping Noah with his training. For this, take Malcolm."

"What?"

"This is the price of his admission. That he helps the Pack."

"Later. This—"

"This is the perfect opportunity. With four of you there to watch him. Take Malcolm. Test him and get this over with."

We truncated the Pack meeting, bringing the others up to speed quickly, and then telling Nick, Reese and Malcolm to grab their bags.

"You want…me?" Malcolm said.

"Not particularly," I said. "But as long as you're here, you might as well join us as extra muscle in case it's a trap."

"Oh, there's no 'in case' about it. You're about to walk into an ambush, Elena."

"It's only an ambush if we don't see it coming. We'll stop by your hotel for your things."

"I drove up this morning with what I have on me, presuming I'd be headed home tonight."

"Then I guess you'll be stocking up on toothpaste and deodorant at the gas station. Go get in my car."

Six

WE DROVE TO West Virginia, Malcolm with me and Clay, and Nick driving his car with Reese as shotgun. It was that or take two flights and still drive three hours to Lonny Cain's place.

Driving meant we had enough time to stop at eleven and grab a few hours sleep. We didn't want to be walking into Lonny Cain's forest at two in the morning. We'd arranged to meet Davis in a diner outside the nearest town at five. At 4:45, we found him already there, chugging coffee and gazing anxiously out the front window.

Davis looked like a Cain, which is to say he was big and brawny and not about to win a beauty contest anytime soon. He wasn't as downright ugly as some Cains, but only a touch to the negative side of average. He also looked a little less rough-around-the-edges than most of his family. Nick jokes that whenever he meets a Cain, he hears the banjos from *Deliverance* in the background. Davis looked more like a college football player, dressed in jeans, sneakers and a pullover, with short brown hair and a clean-shaven square face. The clothing all looked new, as if he really had been on the run since Friday night and bought more presentable attire for us. Or as if he was just smart enough to look as if he had.

We came in the side door, and he didn't spot us until we were a few feet from his table. Then he rose quickly, hand extended. He had that hand aimed at Clay for only a second before he swung it my way instead.

"Ms. Michaels, right?"

"Elena is fine." I motioned for him to sit.

We'd left Nick and Reese in Nick's car, so it wouldn't seem like we expected a trap. Malcolm had accompanied us, and Davis glanced at him, expecting an introduction. Malcolm's lips tightened, annoyed that an introduction was required. Forgetting exactly how long he'd been out of the game.

"This is a new recruit," I said.

"New?" Davis gave a nervous laugh. "Guess there's no age limit, huh?"

Malcolm's lips tightened more.

"No, that's cool," Davis said. "The older we get, the more we need a support system, right? It's great that the Pack does that. And it's great that you're still getting out and keeping active."

There wasn't even a hint of mockery in Davis's voice, which only made it all the more fun to watch.

"Perhaps a proper introduction is in order, Elena," Malcolm said, his voice deceptively soft.

"Sure. Davis, this is Malcolm."

Not a hint of recognition sparked in the boy's eyes. He just extended a hand and said, "Pleased to meet you, sir."

"Malcolm Danvers," Malcolm said.

"Danvers? Oh, you're family then. That's cool. So you're…" He looked at Clay. "No, you're adopted, which means Malcolm is a relative of Jeremy's."

"I'm his father," Malcolm said, barely able to get the words out.

"Father? Shit. You're still—I mean, you must be even older than you—I mean, you look good for your age."

And that was it. Davis Cain had no idea who Malcolm was. Which really put things into perspective. Time marches on. One minute you're the terror of the mutt world, and the next, they don't even bother telling their kids horror stories about you.

"I can also *fight* good for my age," Malcolm said. "Perhaps you'd like to challenge this *old man*."

Davis smiled and shook his head.

"Yeah," Clay said. "Better not. We wouldn't want you to break a hip."

I choked on a laugh and covered it by motioning to the server for coffee. Davis said, "Nah, actually, I wasn't smiling because of that. I just meant that I'm not foolhardy enough to accept. Despite your age, you're obviously in good shape. The Pack wouldn't let you come out on missions if you couldn't hold your own. I don't have nearly the experience you do, so I'd rather not get my ass kicked."

"By a geriatric werewolf," Clay said, and I shot him a partially-disapproving look. But only partially.

"Okay," I said. "Now that we're done with the introductions, I want you to tell me the whole story again, Davis. From the start. For Malcolm's benefit."

Davis fingered his coffee cup and said nothing. The server arrived and topped it up, filled ours and left with Clay's order for "bacon, toast, eggs—just bring what you've got, enough for the table." Even after she was gone, Davis stayed quiet.

"Is there a problem?" I asked.

"I..." He looked me in the eyes. "I'd rather you just came out and said you don't believe me. Ask me to tell my story again so you can read my body language when I do. So you can look in my face when I do. Maybe I'm not supposed to say that, but I want to cut through the crap. You don't trust Cains.

You don't trust 'mutts,' as you call us. You don't trust me. Just say it and move on."

"Okay," Clay said. "We're saying it. And having said it, we want your phone on the table."

"Why—? Oh, so I can't call my uncle and cousin and warn them you suspect a trap. I really wish I could call them. Wish to hell I could. But…" He set his phone on the table. "There. Okay, so I was driving back from a date and ran out of gas. I'd stupidly forgotten to fill up in town, so I had a five-mile hike…"

*

"Fuck," Clay said, as soon as we walked into the forest behind the Cain cottage. We could already smell rotting corpses. While properly setting up this trap would have involved haul-ing in a dead body for the smell, that was a little more ingenuity than we expected from the Cains. Also, judging by the smell, it wasn't just a random corpse stolen from a morgue. With every step we took, the stench got worse, and it was a testament to the remoteness of the location that no humans had stumbled over the scene yet.

When we finally drew close enough to see the bodies, I deeply regretted scarfing down that greasy breakfast. I was used to bloody deaths. This? This was so much worse.

It was exactly as Davis had described. His uncle and his cousin had been shot, skinned and strung up while they were still in wolf form. Contrary to popular lore, we don't Change back on death. Die a wolf, stay a wolf. Which is what happened here. Two werewolves, hung up like sides of beef in a slaughterhouse. That's what they looked like—fly-covered sides of beef, and it was that thought, more than anything, that made my stomach lurch.

And if that wasn't enough? One of the two was missing more than his hide. He'd been castrated.

"Well, that's two less mutts to worry about," Malcolm said.

I spun on him.

"What? The boy's over there." He waved at Davis, twenty feet away. "Couldn't stomach it."

"Yes," I said. "In the normal world, people don't really like seeing the corpses of their relatives."

"Tell that to funeral homes."

I glared at him. "My point wasn't whether the boy can hear you."

"What was it then? That I was being insensitive? Is that what the Pack's come to now?" He snorted. "I suppose that's what *his* leadership got you, isn't it? Opening up the Pack to traitors and werewolf daughters. Appointing a woman Alpha and making the Pack an international joke. And now you cry over dead mutts."

Clay hit him. It happened so fast even I didn't see it coming. No growl of warning. No snarl. Not even a glare. One second, Clay was standing there, impassively listening. The next Malcolm was on the ground, rubbing his jaw, and Clay's expression hadn't changed.

Malcolm leaped up and rushed him. Clay feinted, grabbed him by the back of the jacket and slammed him into a tree, pinning him there.

"I put you down for disrespecting the Alpha," he said, leaning into Malcolm's ear. "This is for fighting back. I know it's been a while, so here's a reminder. I'm her enforcer. If I punish you, what do you do?"

A moment of silence. Then Malcolm ground out between his teeth, "Take it."

"Louder."

"I take it."

He threw Malcolm aside. "Elena isn't crying over dead mutts. She's expressing proper respect for dead werewolves who, as far as we are aware, did nothing to earn our disrespect beyond being mutts. I know you're having a hard time holding your tongue, Malcolm. You respect us about as much as you respect those dead mutts. But every time you insult us, you embarrass yourself, because this is the Pack you chose to join. Which means all your snarling sounds like the yipping of some little dog that just wants to remind the world he's still here. That he's still relevant. Here's a tip, Malcolm." He shot a meaningful look Davis's way. "No one knows you anymore. No one cares. All the yipping in the world won't change that. If you honestly want someone to care, try being a wolf they'll want to remember."

Clay turned to me and nodded at the corpses. "Cut them down?"

"Please," I said.

He said to Malcolm, "Since their condition obviously doesn't bother you, I'm sure you won't mind holding them while I cut." ⌐

Seven

I CALLED NICK AND Reese in. They'd followed us to the cottage and had been patrolling the nearby forest for signs of trouble, but since we were now reasonably sure we hadn't been led into a trap, I brought them in and introduced them to Davis.

We buried the Cains. That's harsh—burying them in the forest, no marker for their graves. But it's what we expect as werewolves. We are unlikely to die at home in our beds, and even if we do, there isn't going to be a service and an obituary in the paper. Given the state of the Cains' bodies, we didn't dare load them into the trunks and drive them elsewhere for burial, as much as I'd have preferred that for safety.

"Shot as wolves, skinned and strung up like wild game, and then dumped in graves like discarded animal carcasses," I muttered to Clay as we walked back ahead of the others.

"Yeah," he said. "Helluva thing. They might have been mutts but..."

"That's what the killers treated them like: vermin," Nick said, overhearing as he caught up. "I'm sure you guys are already thinking it, but I'm beginning to suspect we didn't squash that bounty hunt problem quite as well as we thought."

Clay had mentioned that possibility right after Davis's call. The bounty hunt was a case Nick and Vanessa handled shortly after they met. We'd actually stumbled on it, quite literally. Nick and Vanessa had been hunting Malcolm, only to discover he was also being hunted by supernaturals looking to collect a bounty. It seemed someone had decided werewolves were indeed vermin, and offered a reward for kills.

Nick and Vanessa had tracked the bounties to a wealthy half-demon who claimed his wife had been murdered by a werewolf. Turned out "murdered" was an exaggeration, considering she was still alive and shacked up with the mutt. We'd let Vanessa handle the rest, given that the guy really wasn't a fan of our kind. He'd backed down pretty fast, especially when two Cabals sent him cease-and-desist messages. If he rattled the wolf cages, they'd hold him personally responsible for any counter-attacks against supernaturals. They may also have frozen his assets, which was probably far more effective as a deterrent. He rescinded the bounties, having apparently never paid out a single one, when the prospective hunters discovered werewolves aren't easy prey.

Had something happened to change his mind? Did he wake up one morning, look at his wife's empty side of the bed, say, "Screw the Cabals," and put out the bounties again? Possible, but sadly, he was far from the only supernatural who saw us as little more than dangerous vermin.

Back at the house, Clay and I checked the scents on the porch. Davis said he thought he smelled a werewolf. My nose is the best in the Pack, but it'd been two days and the scents had faded. While I definitely picked up werewolf, three of them had lived here. I committed all the scents to memory and went inside.

My nose confirmed that Davis had figured out the story as best it could be determined. Someone had come to the door. The Cains saw five men with guns and knew it wasn't the local rotary club trying to sign them up. They ran out the back and Changed. Then they were hunted, with their killers never setting foot inside the house.

When I finished inside the house, I walked to Davis, who was standing by the road. We'd given his phone back after burying his uncle and cousin, and he was checking his messages, which involved some fancy footwork out here, to find a spot with signal and then position the phone just right to catch it.

As I approached, he was cursing under his breath.

"Can't get a signal?"

"No, I did. I'm just not hearing back from Uncle Theo."

We hadn't been the first people he'd called after finding Lonny and Curtis. That honor went to Theo Cain, clan patriarch. But Theo was down in Mexico with a few of his "boys"—sons and grandsons—and Davis hadn't been able to get in touch.

"Where'd you say he was again?" I asked.

"Mexico. I don't know exactly where. He left a message with Uncle Lonny, saying he got some kind of job. A good-paying one that would take him south of the border for a couple of weeks. He was grabbing a few of the boys and heading out that night."

"When was that?"

"Thursday."

I glanced at Clay, walking over to join us.

"Yeah," Davis said. "I know. It'd be hard for anyone to target Uncle Theo at home. But on the road? He's not nearly as careful. Not if he's chasing a big payday."

"Do you at least know if they *got* to Mexico?"

He shook his head. "They were meeting their contact on this side of the border. El Paso, I think. That's all I know."

"Give me a list of all the phone numbers you know—and any aliases—and I'll have someone start hunting."

✎

LOGAN AND KATE both play video games. They're particularly fond of the role-playing ones, where you form a "party"
and go off adventuring. Sometimes, I feel like I live in those
games. Especially when it comes to juggling my "party." That's
what I did next. Swap out Reese, so he and Maddie could track
Theo Cain online. Keep Nick with us, because he had experience with the bounty hunt quest. Add Vanessa, because she's
the one who dealt with the bounty hunter. And then remove
Malcolm as backup enforcer, replacing him with Karl.

"Jeremy says keep Malcolm," I grumbled as I got off the
phone. "Remind me again who is actually Alpha here?"

Clay wisely didn't answer that. The truth is that Jeremy's
advice was just that: advice. I followed it because he had a
point. I just didn't like to admit that.

"If I didn't know better," I said, "I'd say he's secretly hoping
Malcolm does something bad enough we have to kill him."

"We can only hope," Clay said, as we headed to join
the others.

I called and asked Vanessa to join us. I can't order her;
she isn't Pack. The "mates" of my wolves expect to be given
tasks and be respected as equals, though, which I'm happy to

do. Malcolm snarked about the Pack changing. It has. Gone are the days when the guys had human girlfriends who never knew they were werewolves. Back then, if you had a daughter, you left her behind with her mother and moved on. If you had a son, you took the baby and left the mother to grieve. No one is sorry to see that time pass. The Pack is comprised of families, as it always has been. Those families just happen to now include wives, girlfriends and daughters, and we're stronger for it.

I knew Vanessa might not be able to help on this. Her job comes first, which is what differentiates her from full Pack members. But when I called, she'd already been in touch with her boss—Rhys—to juggle next week's duties if I needed her.

That led to another problem.

When Vanessa and Nick had been hunting Malcolm, she'd underestimated him. He'd pinned her and given her a choice—he could kill her or break her neck and leave her paralyzed.

Vanessa's no damsel in distress. She's a half-demon former FBI agent who leads a squad of supernatural operatives. In that moment, with Malcolm, she'd been helpless in a way she hadn't been in a very long time. I know exactly what that was like. You think you've overcome your weaknesses and welded on your armor good and tight and then someone finds the chink and rips it off in a heartbeat. You don't forget that. You just don't.

That moment haunted her. That *choice* haunted her. She told me that she would have chosen death, and that makes her feel weak, as if for all her strength, she'd have folded in the face of a "real" challenge—a physical one.

Nick doesn't know about the choice. I'm sure he suspects there was more to the encounter than Malcolm taking Vanessa down. But she knows he can't deal with Malcolm objectively if he realizes how badly he hurt her. So it's our secret—hers and mine.

Once again, I wanted to minimize the strain of a Malcolm meeting. Now I needed her on this mission, with him. If I had my way, they'd spend as little time together as possible. ⌒

Eight

E WERE STILL in West Virginia, at a motel, making plans for the next step.

"All right then," I said. "Reese? You'll drive home in Nick's car. Take Davis, and find him a place to lie low. Ohio might be best." I looked at Malcolm. "Actually, give Davis your keys. He can stay at your place for a few days."

"I am not letting a Cain brat—"

"I can hear you," Davis said.

"Yeah, mate, he knows," Reese said. "He's just an ass. Malcolm, you heard the boss. Hand over your keys."

"The hell I'm—"

"Who pays the rent on your apartment?" I asked.

"Temporarily. I'll be finding work—"

"Wonderful. And until you do, that's our apartment, and Davis needs to lie low for a while."

"I don't want to lie low," Davis said. "My family was murdered. I think I deserve the chance to help find their killers. While I might not be the best fighter around, I'm big, and that's usually enough with humans. I'll make better backup than..." He looked at Malcolm. "Yes, you're probably a better fighter, but I'm bigger and younger, so to humans, I'm the intimidating one. And from what I've seen, Elena and Clayton can trust me more than they can trust you."

"Good on ya, kid." Reese looked at me. "Your call, boss."

"All right," I said. "You can come along for this next part, Davis. But I expect you to obey orders and do as you're told."

"I'm a Cain," he said. "We might not be a Pack, but we're as close to it as you can get. I know the drill."

*

REESE LEFT BY plane instead because I was not squeezing four guys in my car for a five-hour drive. We grabbed a few hours of shuteye before we left. And unfortunately, Clay and I did nothing more than sleep. Being away from the kids should have meant an opportunity to enjoy some private time. But we had one room for five of us, with two double beds and a chair. Sharing that room with two werewolves we didn't trust meant Nick, Clay and I slept in shifts. It wasn't exactly a restful night.

We were up at three for the drive to Cincinnati to meet Vanessa's flight. Nick drove his car and took Davis. We got Malcolm again, who slept for most of the ride. I resisted any urge to comment on the elderly needing more rest.

Clay and I took advantage of Malcolm's sleep to talk for most of the trip. It's been fifteen years since we got back together after a courtship that crashed in flames—which tends to happen when your fiancé bites you and turns you into a werewolf. It took me a decade to get over that, to understand it had been an act of panic and desperation rather than cold calculation.

Still, after fifteen years, you'd think we'd have run out of things to talk about. We hadn't. We juggle family life and Pack lives while attempting to retain some semblance of careers. We might be together almost constantly, but it's rare to have uninterrupted hours where we can just talk. Because, let's be honest, if there is an uninterrupted hour alone, we find other things to do.

On that drive, we mostly discussed work. Clay's an anthropologist. I'm...well, I'm a journalist by trade but these days, even making part-time freelance hours is difficult. I'm sure as hell not going to write content for an online blog and be grateful if they pay me a penny a word. Some freelance work still lands on my desk. Mostly, I make my own, investigating topics that interest me, and seeing what I can sell. And yes, when you combine that with Clay's scholarly articles and a few weeks of lecturing a year, we barely earn enough to pay Stonehaven's bills. But Jeremy has more money than he'll ever spend and a girlfriend who hardly needs his income to support her. Clay and I only keep our jobs to give us a sliver of life outside the Pack. But the Pack *is* our life, and our jobs leave us free to devote as much time to it as it requires.

NICK AND I waited for Vanessa right outside the arrivals gate. He met her with a kiss that lasted long enough for me to say, "You're blocking exiting traffic, guys. Get a hotel for lunch and order room service."

Vanessa laughed and said, "Sorry." Her husky voice held a bit of a tremor, and I knew that wasn't from the kiss, just as I knew the kiss had been Nick's way of calming her nerves—a reminder that he thought she was amazing and could easily handle Malcolm.

"So how's it going?" she asked as we started walking.

"He behaved himself during the Meet. Before that, he insulted pretty much everyone. Except Jaime and Madison. He just leered at them."

"Which is insulting enough."

I smiled. "Exactly what I said. So that's what you have to look forward to. Leering." *And hopefully nothing more.*

"Do you want to take off ahead with Nick? Postpone this a little longer?"

"Is that what you'd want?"

Which was all she needed to say, and that's why we get on so well. Two women who don't back down from a fight, even when, maybe, they should.

We returned to where we'd left Clay, Davis and Malcolm sitting in a quiet spot. As they rose, I said, "Malcolm? This is Vanessa."

She strode past and put out her hand. "We've met," she said, before he could get that in, leaving him standing with his mouth partly open. She turned to Davis. "And *we* have not. Vanessa Callas."

Davis shook her hand, I introduced him and that was that. Situation handled. Yes, unlike Jeremy and Karl and Clay, Vanessa wasn't over her history with Malcolm. But it wasn't about him. What scared her was the question he'd raised and the doubts it cast on her image of herself. Like them, she could handle this. I was starting to feel as if everyone could, except the woman who'd had to bring him back into their lives.

Nine

AN HOUR LATER, we were walking into the reception area of a downtown Cincinnati high-rise. The office looked very classy, all white surfaces and chrome, without even a hint of what kind of business you'd find inside.

We'd left Malcolm, Nick and Davis on guard duty, covering the elevator and stairwells, in case our quarry bolted. Vanessa led Clay and me to the reception desk. "Vanessa Callas to see Mr. Marsh."

The receptionist checked her book. "I don't see your—"

"It's an open invitation. I work with an agency that Mr. Marsh has been very keen to retain. I was in town with two of our actors and thought we'd pop by. Just ring him. Tell him the name. He'll see me."

The receptionist looked dubious, but she placed the call and then said, "Mr. Marsh will see you immediately. Second door on your left."

"Actors?" Clay said as we walked. "What exactly does Marsh do?"

"Makes films," I said.

He gave me a look. "Yeah, I figured that. What kind of films?"

"Well, let's just say you don't need to do much acting. But he may ask you to drop your jeans for a measurement." I glanced over. "Just go with it."

"What? Wait—"

"Too late," Vanessa murmured, as she rapped on the door and pushed it open without waiting for a response.

Marsh stood with his back to us, flipping through a pile of stills. Clay got one glance at those pictures and shot me a look that said we would discuss this later. I pantomimed the jean-dropping and mouthed, *Remember: don't break character.* He shot me the finger.

"I hope this is important, Vanessa," Marsh said, attention on his stills. "I know I owe your agency for getting me out of that bounty hunt mess, but I really would have been happier paying in cash. I don't like owing favors." He turned. "And I don't appreciate you showing up here with some story about bringing actors…"

He saw us and stopped. His gaze flicked up me and down Clay. "You brought me actors." A more critical once-over. "They're a little old, but there's a market for maturity. They have a good look." He turned to Clay. "So, how big—"

"Elena Michaels," I said, because as amusing as the ruse was, I'd have to spend the very long return trip in a car with Clay. "Alpha of the American Pack. This is my husband, Clayton Danvers."

For a moment, Marsh seemed about to ask if this meant we wouldn't do a porn movie for him. Then he blinked. His mouth opened. It shut. He turned sharply on Vanessa, "You brought—"

"Don't worry," I said. "We're house-broken. Now sit."

"I—"

"Sit," I said, pointing at the chair as Clay moved forward.

Marsh sat. To Vanessa, he said, "I am filing a serious complaint with your boss, girlie."

"Girlie?" She laughed. "I haven't heard that one in about twenty years. Rhys knew I was bringing Elena here. If you feel the need to verify that, please do so. Just understand that he really hates it when someone suggests he's lost control of his operatives."

"Then I will remember his lack of professional respect, letting you come here under false pretenses—"

"I'm an undercover agent," Vanessa said. "False pretenses is in my job description."

"—and bringing these two into my office, knowing very well how I feel about their kind."

"Yes, we know," I said. "Your wife screwed off with a werewolf and now you're pissed at the entire race. But it happens. First, there's the animal attraction thing. Some women go for that. Add in the delayed aging and the constant training for challenge fights and well…" I motioned at Clay. "It makes for a package that's hard to resist. I wouldn't take it personally."

Marsh glowered at me. "If you came to insult me—"

"I came to help," I said. "We were doing a review of our Pack records and realized there was an omission in our file on your bounty hunt. You neglected to tell Vanessa the name of the werewolf your wife hooked up with."

He bristled. "I don't see how that's any of your business."

"All right, if you feel that way, I won't push. But given the trouble he caused, I thought we should pay him a visit. Have a little chat."

"Punish him?"

"He could have been responsible for werewolf deaths, all because he couldn't keep his pants zipped."

"Ramon," he said quickly. "I'm not sure of the last name. He was Mexican."

"Ramon Santos," I said.

"Right. That's it."

I knew who Santos was. Spanish, not Mexican. From one of the oldest werewolf families, a branch of which used to be Pack...and one of whom had led the rebellion Karl had joined.

Ramon himself had never been Pack. Him and a buddy had been responsible for some murders a few years ago and blamed Reese, which is how we found him. Ramon's buddy, Liam, was dead—not by us, though I'd never quite figured out the whole story there. But Liam had died and Ramon had gone into hiding. He hadn't caused us trouble since. That meant if we ran into him, we would indeed need to punish him for the murders. But we weren't actively hunting him.

As for sleeping with another man's wife, that isn't considered a crime worthy of the Pack's attention or we'd be a whole lot busier. I wanted the name because I'd wondered if the guy could have been a Cain. That would have provided Marsh with a motive. Call off the bounty on werewolves, stew about it for a few years, and then try again, specifically targeting the family that had done him wrong.

"Is she still with Ramon?" I asked.

"Nah, he cut her loose two years ago. She tried crawling back to me. I offered to give her a job instead." He snickered. "There's a market for what she likes. Just get a nice big dog—"

"So she's moved on," Vanessa cut in. "Is it possible she found another werewolf?"

"Not unless you've got one who's also a four-hundred-pound adult entertainment director named Bernie."

"That'd be a no," Vanessa said.

"Let's go back to that bounty business, Mr. Marsh," I said.

"Look, like I told everyone at the time, I was just blowing off steam. I was pissed off about Cindy, and you know how it is." He glanced at Clay for support.

"Your wife screws around so you kill everyone remotely connected to the guy?" Clay said.

"No one actually *died*," Marsh said.

"About the nature of the bounty," I said. "How were they supposed to prove they killed a werewolf? Bring you a wolf skin?"

"What?" His face screwed up. "How the hell would they do that?"

"Kill him while he's in wolf form."

"By following the guy around until he Changed? That's a little complicated. Then after he was dead for a while, he'd Change back and they'd have a human skin. That's disgusting. Hell, even a wolf pelt is disgusting."

"What *did* you demand?"

He threw up his hands. "Proof. Just proof. I wasn't exactly thinking it through." He paused, thinking. "One group asked if I wanted the head or something. I said that was gross. And unsanitary. I told them to just bring me pictures of the trophy." He glanced at us. "I mean the, uh, body."

"Did anyone else suggest they'd bring back a skin if they killed one?"

"Hell, no. No one suggested anything. These guys weren't well-organized. It really wasn't a big deal. It wasn't like they had a chance of actually bagging—killing—a werewolf. It was more like a game than an actual hunt. Which is why no one died."

"The more you harp on that," Vanessa said, "the more you're just reminding Elena and Clay that you put bounties on werewolves. Bounties on them, on their children..."

"What? Kids? *No!*"

"Werewolves have children, Mr. Marsh. Those children are werewolves, and fulfilled your criteria, whatever their age. You put bounties on all of them. So stop backpedaling, and just answer Elena's questions."

"Thank you," I said. "You ended those bounties two years ago—"

"Two years and six months. Actually, even longer than that. I pretended to stall because I didn't like being ordered around, but I withdrew the bounties right away."

"The point is that you withdrew them. The question is whether anyone argued with that. Anyone who might have kept hunting even without a bounty."

"Guys argued, sure. Demanded I pay for their gear and their travel. It was a financial nightmare."

"Which, as I recall," Vanessa said, "you paid off by promising them copies of all your movies."

"Hey, that's not cheap. A lot of them demanded DVDs. That requires shipping."

"Back to the question…"

"Right. So, yes, some complained and demanded reimbursement. But they realized they weren't going to collect a bounty and the movies were a great consolation prize."

"They do know they can get porn on the Internet, right?" Vanessa said. "Free?"

Marsh sniffed. "Sure, if they want to see a couple college kids screwing for a computer cam. No storyline. Nonexistent production values. You get what you pay for."

I asked again, "Did you get *any* sense that anyone was committed to the hunt, regardless of payout?"

"No. Like I said, it was too hard. They were the kind of guys who hunt in wildlife preserves. They were happy with the movies."

"Have you heard anyone *else* offering bounties?"

He hesitated.

"Anyone else wanting to kill werewolves at all," Clay said. "Either specific ones or werewolves in general."

"Well, a guy did pay me a visit a few months ago, asking about my experience with the bounties, seeing if I could provide the names of any particularly skilled hunters. I said *skilled* wasn't the word to describe any of the men who tried to take me up on the offer. Now, if you want details, I'm happy to give them, on the condition that it wipes out my obligation to Vanessa's employer."

"It will," she said. "On the condition that what you provide doesn't turn out to be bullshit to get us out of your office."

"It's not," he said.

"Then we'd be square." She took out her phone, hit speed dial and handed it to Marsh. "You can speak to Rhys yourself." ⌒

Ten

I'D ASKED MARSH whether he'd heard of anyone targeting specific werewolves or werewolves in general. The answer was: neither. Not an individual or the species as a whole, but rather one family: the Cains.

Not that he knew the name. He claimed that if he did, he'd have notified Vanessa to pass along the message, which was bullshit, but I made it clear that if he didn't want to be on the shit-list of an entire species, he'd damned well better make some attempt to foster goodwill with the Pack in future. It was obvious he really didn't want to be on our shit-list. So he was as forthcoming as he could be now that he got the chance.

He honestly didn't know the family name, mostly because he hadn't cared to ask. From what he'd gleaned, it was a large family. And someone wanted the bloodline thinned, if not wiped out completely.

As for why the Cains were targets, again he didn't know and hadn't asked. He'd only picked up that much in the course of the conversation, which had been strictly, "Hey, I know you had a bounty on werewolves a few years back—any tips you can give?"

"Biggest tip I gave him?" Marsh said. "Stay the hell away from the werewolves. It's not like the old days, when no one cared. Werewolves have connections now." He stopped, realizing who he was talking to. "Which is good. Open communication helps all supernaturals."

"But it also means you can't get away with putting down werewolves like rabid dogs."

"Yeah." He cleared the note of regret from his throat. "Which is also good. Believe me, I've come to a much better understanding—"

"You've come to the understanding that you can't fuck with werewolves—regrettably," Clay said. "We get it. Move on."

"I told this guy it wasn't a good idea because of your, uh, connections with the Cortez and Nast Cabals. Well, on top of the fact that it's wrong, which I also told him—"

"You warned him off the idea," I said. "And his response?"

"He laughed. He said he wasn't concerned about the

Cabals. If they found out, they'd look away, under the circumstances."

"What circumstances?"

"I have no idea."

"Could he have been *with* a Cabal?" Vanessa pressed. "Hired by one?"

"I didn't ask. After what happened before, the less I knew about this, the less trouble I could get in."

"Did you give him anything?" I asked.

"Some basic do's and don'ts. Nothing earth-shattering, but the guy was paying for my time, so I had to put on a show. I told him hunting werewolves isn't nearly as easy as it seems, because they're better hunters than any guys you send after them." He looked at me, as if expecting a pat on the head for his compliment.

"And his response?"

"Just that he knew all about werewolves. I figured he must have hunted them in the Old Country."

"Old Country?"

"Mother Russia. Guy had an accent you could carve with a knife."

"He said he was Russian?"

"No, but I have an ear for accents."

"Is there anything else you can tell us about him?"

Marsh opened a desk drawer, rifled around and pulled out

a piece of paper. He handed it to me.

"Does this help?" he asked.

On the paper was a name and a phone number.

WE WALKED DOWN the stairs of Marsh's building. Sixteen flights because it was lunch hour and *someone* didn't like crowded elevators.

We were almost down when Reese called.

"Just the person I wanted to talk to," I said. "I need you or Madison to run a name and phone number."

"And I was just calling *you* about a name and phone number. Carter Cain."

It took a moment to place the name. He was Theo's grandson, one of the younger Cains, maybe twenty-one, twenty-two. Davis thought he might have gone with Theo to Mexico. Davis had tried calling and hadn't gotten an answer, which might only mean Carter was ignoring him. As Davis said, *"He's kind of a dick."*

"Did you track Carter down?" I asked Reese.

"His phone, yes. It was last used outside El Paso."

"Which is where Davis thought Theo was supposed to meet his contact for the job."

"That was Sunday morning. It hasn't been used since.

Theo Cain and Nate Cain's phones were last used outside Houston on Friday."

"Which is where they were living. Suggesting they left their phones behind."

Nate was another grandson—Carter's cousin and about ten years older. *"Not exactly a genius but a decent guy,"* was Davis's summary. Which pretty much summed up the two ends of the spectrum for Cains—dumb but decent guys and total dicks.

"I also got an El Paso hit for Ford Cain," Reese said.

That was the mutt Clay and I had encountered on our honeymoon, the other young Cain we let walk away. Well, *run* away, in Ford's case, and not because he seemed to fall on the dumb-but-decent end of the scale. Ford was definitely a dick. But he made his relatives look like Mensa material, which meant he was a dick without the brains to be dangerous.

Reese continued. "Ford last used his phone in El Paso on Saturday. Two calls to a local number. Maybe their contact. Carter sent about twenty texts that day alone, apparently to friends back home."

"Ah. Definitely a cell-phone generation kid," I said. "So that sudden stop in calls…"

"If he was Pack, I'd think he just turned it off to hide his location while he goes on a mission."

"That's probably why Theo and Nate left theirs behind.

But Carter said screw that. If he's not using his now, it suggests he's no longer able to. Which could mean Theo found and took it away..."

"Or something worse."

I had the feeling the answer was *something worse.*

Eleven

*E*L PASO WAS not a short car ride away—or even a manageably long one. This required air transportation.

We left Vanessa in Cincinnati. Tracking the Cains really was werewolf business, and tracking the guy who'd visited Marsh was more *her* type of business. We went out for lunch and then dropped her off at an upscale hotel with good room service, where she would hole up with her phone and her laptop, keeping in touch with Reese and Madison while they tracked Marsh's visitor.

We arrived in El Paso just past the dinner hour, local time. Which meant a stop for Texas BBQ. Hey, we needed energy for the hunt, and it didn't look as if there'd be many fast food restaurants where we were going. Reese had tracked the Cains' phones to "outside El Paso," which was the best our technology could do. Vanessa had access to better, and by the time we landed, she'd sent us exact coordinates for Carter and Ford's phones. They were well outside the city, in the middle of nowhere. Or that's where she picked up Ford's phone. Carter's last location was about half a mile away, before the signal had vanished, the phone either out of battery or turned off.

It was dark by the time we reached the area. That was what we wanted, though. The land here was too open for tracking in daylight.

We split up—Nick and Davis stayed with me, while Clay and Malcolm drove the rental SUV further, to approach from a different angle. We were aiming for Ford's phone. It was closer than the last known location for Carter's.

As Nick, Davis and I walked along a dusty path, Davis said, "I feel like I'm on the set of a Western." He glanced to the side. "And, on cue, a tumbleweed rolls past. That *is* a tumbleweed, isn't it?"

"Seems like it."

He scanned the landscape. "It's pretty out here, in a desolate kind of way. Not like the forest. It's so quiet." He paused. "Which probably means I should be, too."

"No, you're fine. It's quiet enough that anyone around will hear us coming, talking or not. And we've got two miles to go.

We'll hike until we're out of sight of the road and then find a place to Change. Which you don't have to, if it's a problem."

"No, I can. It just might take a while. I was, uh, a bit of a late bloomer."

"How old?" Nick asked.

"Eighteen."

"Beat me then. It's not a big deal, even if I'm sure everyone razzed you about it."

"Yeah, they still do. Especially Carter—who was barely two months younger when he first Changed. Nate tells me to ignore it. He was twenty his first time. At family gatherings, when the others would Change for a run or a hunt, Nate would stay behind with me." Davis peered into the night. "I hope he's all right. I hope they all are. They must be. No one could get the jump on all four of them." He looked at me. "Right?"

"Five men, even with guns, aren't going to be able to take out four werewolves. I don't know what happened out here but..." I wanted to say it can't be that bad. That would be an empty reassurance, though.

"I bet they're already down in Mexico," Davis said. "They met the guy for the job in El Paso, and then came out here for a run and forgot where they left their clothing, phones and all. It's happened before. I always tell them to pay attention to where they undress. But they're in such a rush." He shook his head. "My family."

"Oh, it's not just yours," Nick said. "I seem to recall a time or two when certain Pack members misplaced their clothing because they were in a hurry. Now, they claimed they were in a hurry to *Change*, but I'm pretty sure that wasn't what they were actually undressing for."

"It was once," I said. "*Once*."

"She can't count," he whispered to Davis. "And because she's Alpha, we can't argue with her anymore. Which she *loves*."

Davis smiled and shook his head.

"Ignore him," I said. "He's just hoping I'll forget the times he's misplaced his clothing in the forest. And it wasn't because he was distracted by other things. He just plain forgot."

"Temporarily."

"Not always," I said. "*I* seem to recall an incident about five years ago, in Aspen on a ski trip, where there just happened to be a conveniently located hot tub that saved your ass—and other parts—from frostbite. Except it was a private hot tub. Currently in use. Fortunately, the women in it didn't mind. Then their boyfriends showed up."

"Wait," Davis said to Nick. "Like, for real?"

"It wasn't quite—" Nick began.

"It totally was," I said. "Allow me to tell the story." And so I did, successfully distracting Davis from thoughts of his family until we reached a spot to Change. ⌒

Twelve

AS SOON AS I Changed form, I picked up Clay's scent on the breeze, probably because I was subconsciously searching for it. It's rare these days to Change and not bound out to see him. Or bound out to get trounced by him. Or bound out to trounce him. Since Clay was too far away for that tonight, I settled for trouncing Nick. He appreciated it. I'm sure he did.

We tussled for a few minutes, adjusting to the change of form while we waited for Davis to finish. Then we had to wait a few more minutes for him to get his bearings and recoup his energy. I'm accustomed to that these days. The twins don't need to Change as often as we do—thank God—but we take them out monthly, and they're new enough to it that, like Davis, it takes time to orient themselves and recuperate.

While we waited, Nick and I scouted the desert landscape. For a change of run scenery, you can't do much better than this—the open land and hard-packed earth make the desert the perfect place to just put your ears back, slit your eyes against the dust and run. Which is what Nick and I did after we scouted—tearing back and forth, chasing each other until Davis raced over, looking alarmed, as if we'd stumbled over peyote. And that's when he caught his first good whiff of me in wolf form.

The young werewolf went still, very still, his nostrils quivering, eyes widening. Nick charged and knocked him flying. He pinned Davis, growled and cuffed him. Then he snorted and backed up. Davis rose, head lowered, casting a sheepish glance my way before circling wide onto Nick's other side and staying there as we set out.

And so that was handled—the minor inconvenience of the fact that I smell like a bitch in heat. It can get awkward, but Davis was smart enough and cautious enough that there'd only been that one moment, probably more, "What the hell?" than anything else. Nick's attack had cleared his head and warned him to steer clear until he got over the scent. Which I'm sure he was happy to do, given that I'm old enough to be his mother.

Finding the exact coordinates would be tougher without a GPS in hand, but I knew the direction we needed to head and the approximate distance, so we set out at a lope. I kept picking up speed only to force myself to slow to a more measured pace, one that allowed me to keep looking and sniffing and listening. But what I smelled was Clay. Well, yes, Malcolm and Ford Cain and Theo Cain and two other werewolf trails on the ground, but the only scent that mattered to my brain was Clay's.

When we were close enough to him, I stopped and howled. Being upwind, Clay might need the audio clue to find us. He replied with a yipping bark.

We continued on, periodically communicating with yips and yowls that mimicked coyotes, in case anyone was listening. Those yips told us where the other was as we approached the spot, making sure we didn't barrel into one another, which would defeat the purpose of splitting up. Finally, when we were close enough to hear the other's paws thumping against the earth, we stopped communicating and focused on our target.

That's when the wind shifted, bringing with it a smell that brought Davis to a screeching halt. Then he shot forward, and Nick had to charge after him, leaping on his back and sending him muzzle-first into the dirt. Davis scrambled up and lunged at Nick, snarling. Nick put him down and held him there, jaws around his throat, not clamping, just holding, quietly and patiently waiting for him to get it under control.

As I watched, I realized just how much Nick had changed. How far he'd come from the friend who used to tag along after Clay and me. That guy would have hung back and let me handle the scent issue. He'd have let me handle this, too, because it wouldn't occur to him to jump in. He'd await instructions. Five years of "raising" Noah and Reese, though, meant he had to take initiative, to be the Alpha of their family Pack. Now there wasn't a moment of indecision—Davis was a young werewolf, and he knew how to handle young werewolves. So he did without even glancing my way for confirmation.

Once Davis calmed down, Nick pulled him up by the scruff of the neck. Then he growled a warning before releasing him. I walked over and knocked Davis gently in the shoulder, a canine version of a squeeze on the shoulder, a moment of saying, "I understand, and I'm sorry."

What we smelled in the breeze was exactly what I'd smelled in the woods behind Lonny Cain's house.

I motioned to Nick, telling him to keep Davis here. When I started to walk away, Davis whined. I growled and shook my head.

You're not seeing this. Not if you don't have to.

I approached the scene carefully, well aware I had no one to watch my back. Clay was near, though, which meant it was safe enough. And judging by that smell, whoever had done this was long gone.

I scanned the horizon for something to have hung the bodies from. I spotted a stand of what looked like trees slightly to the east, and veered that way as I crested a small rise—

And nearly jumped off a rocky overhang onto the bodies of two dead werewolves.

The bodies were just on the other side of that rise, as if to hide them from the view of anyone hiking past. Not strung up but staked out. Two werewolves in wolf form, skinned and tied to wooden stakes, lying on their backs with their legs splayed and bound.

As for who they'd been, I had no idea. They were skinned wolves. Worse, having been staked out at ground level left them open to every passing coyote and vulture. They were… Let's just say I was very glad I hadn't let Davis come along.

To figure out which Cains these were, I'd need to find their trail. I was turning away when Clay nearly did the same thing I had—bound over that rise. He saw the two bodies at the last second, twisted, and knocked into me instead. I managed to keep my footing and only bumped against him, a gentle, "Hey, watch it." He licked my muzzle in apology and then rubbed against me in greeting. That's when he remembered what he'd seen as he leapt over the rise. He looked at the Cains and let out a deep, shuddering sigh.

And that was different, too. The Clay I'd met thirty years ago would have snorted and turned aside, as if to say, like Malcolm had earlier, "Two fewer mutts in the world." As for me, thirty years ago I'd have been puking up my BBQ dinner. We all change. We learn. We toughen up. And we grow.

Clay moved on to investigate, getting closer to the corpses than I could have, snuffling around them as he tried to pick up scents. I followed him down.

A shadow passed over me, and I remembered we weren't alone here. I glanced to see Malcolm on the rise. He wasn't looking at the mutts, though. He was staring at me, his nose twitching, chest moving as he inhaled deeply. Clay must have heard that inhalation—he snarled a clear, "Knock it off." Malcolm ignored him. He came down off the rise, blue eyes fixed on me, approaching stiff-legged, tail up.

I growled with my head lowered. Clay snarled louder, the fur on his ruff and along his spine rising. Malcolm just kept coming, the look in his eyes less lust than arrogance, an expression that said this was new, and he was going to check it out, and no one was going to stop him. ⌒

Thirteen

I WOULD HAVE DEALT with Malcolm, but I didn't get the chance. Clay vaulted clear over me and jumped on him, jaws snapping, blood flying. Clay and Malcolm went down, biting and clawing and snarling, frenzied.

This wasn't Nick's gentle warning to Davis. This was full-out rage, more than Malcolm's insolence justified. This was Clay's frustration, pent up over two days of having to deal with him, travel with him, act as if he was just another Pack member. I crouched there, watching for the chance to intervene. As soon as I saw some of that blood spraying from Clay, I lunged.

I cut my lunge short. I had to. Jumping in to help Clay was wrong, as much as every part of me wanted to, not because he couldn't handle himself in a fight, but because this was

Malcolm Danvers. The guy who sliced Vanessa's agent's throat just enough for her to slowly bleed out on a warehouse floor. The guy who'd cut out his ex-partner's tongue for betraying him and then stapled the man's dead wife to the attic ceiling. The guy who'd given Vanessa that choice—that terrible choice—for no crime greater than helping Nick track him down.

I remembered all that, and it took everything I had to avert my lunge and stand my ground and tell myself I was here—I was *right here*—and Malcolm couldn't do any of that to Clay. He *wouldn't* do it—deep down I knew that, but at that moment, what mattered was that he couldn't. The moment this fight showed any signs of turning lethal—for either of them—I'd break it up. Until then, I could only watch.

I was still watching when Nick came running, drawn by the sound of the fight. He raced up the rise, saw the bodies and twisted sharply, snarling at Davis to stay back. Then Nick scrabbled down off the rock and began circling the fight, doing the same thing I was, watching for any sign that it needed to be broken up.

Finally Clay had Malcolm pinned, the older wolf snarling and spitting, bloody froth flicking from his jaws. Clay snarled back, ears flattened, lips curled. Nick and I moved in on either side of Malcolm, flanking him and growling, sending the message, "Stay down or we'll put you down."

Clay backed off. Once he was far enough away, I let Malcolm up. He rose and stalked away, as best he could stalk, limping slightly and leaving a trail of blood. Going to lick his wounds, quite literally. I walked to Clay, who stood a few feet away, his flanks heaving as he struggled to get his temper under control.

I nosed his injuries carefully, making sure they weren't serious. After a minute, he leaned against me and exhaled, and I pushed him down to clean his wounds. He let me for a few minutes, and then rose, pressing against me, nose buried in the fur at my neck, inhaling and exhaling, steadying himself with my scent.

When we separated, we both looked toward the bodies. Reminding ourselves that there was work to be done.

I motioned that I'd go Change back. He grunted, saying he would, too. At the top of the rocky rise he looked in the direction he must have left his clothing. Malcolm's scent on the wind said that was where he'd gone. I nudged Clay, gesturing my muzzle in the other direction, asking him if he wanted to Change with me. He dipped his head in a nod. Malcolm or not, we both preferred that, under the circumstances.

Clay and I returned to where I had left my clothing. When I finished Changing he was already done, sitting with his back to me. I put my hands on his shoulders, being careful not to touch the scratches from the fight. He tugged me to his front.

I put my legs on either side of him and straddled his lap, my arms around his neck.

"I'm sorry," I said.

"I think that's my line."

"No, it's mine. I was so worried about how everyone else would react to Malcolm—Jeremy, Vanessa, Karl—that I forgot those weren't the only people he hurt."

"He never hurt me. I was his golden boy."

"And *that's* what hurt you. He flaunted that in front of Jeremy. That you were the son he wanted, and no matter how obvious you made it that you despised him, it didn't change anything. To him, you were the perfect werewolf. And you had to put up with that and watch him treat Jeremy like shit, because you were forbidden to do anything else."

"Jeremy couldn't let me—"

"Of course he couldn't. That didn't make it hurt any less. Didn't make it any easier, all those years of watching him, unable to do anything about it."

"I used to follow him around when I was young. Stalk him. That was before he decided I was more than just a weird wolf kid. I'd follow him until he got so fed up, he'd leave."

I remembered Kate staring at Malcolm, that unnerving stare that had definitely unsettled him, how Clay had chuckled at it.

Clay had probably preferred those early days, when Malcolm treated him like a freak. Because later... Well, there was that "son I never had" aspect to Malcolm's fixation with Clay as a teen and young man. But from every impression I'd gotten, there was more too, something that reminded me a little too much of when I was a foster kid—the way some of my so-called fathers and brothers looked at me, the way a few of them acted on those impulses. Maybe I'm misinterpreting the situation through the filter of my own experience. But before Clay grew up, Antonio says he got the same treatment from Malcolm, and his comments suggest Malcolm's interest had seemed more than fatherly.

"I'm sorry," I said again.

Clay put his arms around my waist. "No reason to be."

"Yes, I forgot—"

"You didn't forget anything. Of all of them, I have the least reason to complain."

I looked him in the eyes. "I disagree."

He shrugged. "Honestly, I thought the only thing that would bother me was seeing Jeremy go through that. But..."

He rolled his shoulders. "I hate it, darling. I hate every fucking second of it, and I know I shouldn't tell you that because you hate it just as much, and you feel guiltier. But I don't hate the choice you made. I hate the choice *we* had to make."

He pulled me closer, hugging my knees to his sides. "You know what, though? As much as I hate it, the fact that it pisses me off so much shows I needed this. Needed to face him. Needed to get it off my chest."

"Needed to kick the shit out of him?"

He chuckled. "Yeah. That felt good. I know it didn't help matters—"

"I don't care."

"Yeah, but—"

"No, seriously. I don't care. If beating the shit out of him for being disrespectful makes you feel better, kick his ass as often as you want. I'll deal with it. You're putting him in his place, and he needs that."

"That used to be his job," he said, his voice low.

"Hmm?"

"Dominic didn't really have a beta when he was Alpha. He just had an enforcer. The guy he sent out to knock mutts around. The guy who'd knock Pack wolves around, too, when they got out of line. That was Malcolm."

"And just because you're doing the same job—"

He cut me off with a kiss. "I know." He smiled and it was a real one, lighting his eyes. "There was a time when I wondered. Not that I thought I was exactly like him, but maybe more than I wanted to be. Now that he's back, though, I see—really see—what he is. We might have done the same job, but I'm nothing like him."

"No, you're not."

I kissed him, a gentle kiss. When he returned it, though, he pulled me tight against him, the kiss deepening, that hunger igniting, the hunger that was never far below the surface, only waiting for a spark.

When he started to move me onto my back, I said, "Careful, you've been—"

"I'm fine."

"Mmm, no, you've got three scrapes, four puncture wounds—"

"And I don't feel a thing. Unless that's a subtle way of saying, 'Not now, we have work to do.'"

"Since when do I let a little thing like that stop us?"

He laughed, laid me on my back and stretched out over me, still kissing me, and for a while, that's all we did. Deep, hungry kisses, hands sliding over skin, not resting anywhere for more than a moment or two, just touching, feeling, stroking, as if we didn't already know each other's bodies by heart. Then his hands moved to my hips and I wrapped my legs around him, my fingers moving up to his hair, pulling him in closer, kissing him harder as he pushed into me. Slow, measured strokes. No rush, no hurry, as if there was nothing else we needed to do. And right then, there wasn't. Nothing else that mattered as much as this. ⌒

Fourteen

E BROUGHT DAVIS and Nick's clothing back to them. Clay may have been wearing Nick's shirt. Nick may have given a wolf grumble about that.

"Yeah, yeah," Clay said. "I wouldn't have bothered, but Elena smelled hikers. She didn't want to scare the locals."

I shook my head. "I never said *scare*. Remember, you almost got cast in a porn movie yesterday. You just needed to pass the tape-measure test."

Nick snickered—a growling rumble—as he picked up his jeans in his teeth. Davis looked confused, as if he was unsure he was translating human-to-wolf correctly. I waved for them to find a place to Change. While they were gone, Clay and I gave the bodies another look. We were still doing that when Nick returned. We rose just as Malcolm stalked over from the other direction.

Malcolm whipped Clay's clothing at his feet. "Don't you *ever* do that again."

"No," Clay said, grabbing his clothes. "*Anytime* you disrespect the Alpha, you'd better expect that."

Malcolm snorted. "That wasn't about disrespecting the Alpha. It was about me checking out your wife. If you have a problem with jealousy, Clayton—"

"A problem with jealousy would imply I think you had a shot in hell."

"All right, then, you were just being *protective*." Malcolm sneered the last word.

"No, *that* would imply Elena couldn't have taken you down herself. That fight wasn't about sex, Malcolm. It was about disrespect. You've never smelled her in wolf form. It was new. I get that. So I warned you to back off. She warned you to back off. You refused to back off. Anytime you disobey both of us like that, I'm going to kick your ass." Clay stepped closer. "And, yeah, I'm going to enjoy it. So if you don't want your ass kicked, don't give me an excuse."

"All right," I said. "The next step is to see if we can follow the trails of our killers. Yes, that would have been easier in wolf form, but we got a little distracted there. So let's focus on—"

"Can someone explain what we're doing here?" Malcolm said.

Clay gave a warning growl.

"No, really," Malcolm said. "You seem to have yourself a new, *progressive* Pack, so I should be able to speak my mind."

"Actually, no," Nick said. "Considering that whatever comes out of your mouth is unfailingly idiotic, *you* have to stick to the old ways. Shut up, Malcolm. Please."

"I understood checking on the boy's uncle and cousin," Malcolm said. "Make sure the Cains weren't trying to trap us. They weren't. Even then, I understood the need to investigate—if someone's skinning wolves, the Pack has to take an interest, in case they turn on us next. But from what I understand, the only ones being targeted are Cains. So…?"

"Who gives a fuck?" Clay said. "We do. Not because we're responsible for mutts. Not because we particularly care…" His gaze shifted to Davis, coming up the rise, dressed and sweating from the exertion of the Change. I motioned for Davis to stay where he was, reminding him not to come closer to the bodies.

Clay continued, "We care because someone is targeting werewolves, and we can't allow that. It's the principle of the thing."

"Is that what she tells you?" Malcolm hooked his thumb at me.

"Yeah," Clay said, "because obviously I'm unable to think for myself. I'm such a pushover."

"Back in my day—"

"Oh, please," Nick said. "Do you even realize how you sound? Like one of those old men on his porch grumbling about how the world has changed." He walked closer to Malcolm. "Guess what? It has."

"This isn't your daddy's world, Malcolm. It isn't even *your* world. That time has passed. The Pack can't just skim the newspapers for mutts on killing sprees. These days, two man-eating cases a continent apart can be linked. Hell, some kid catches us Changing and puts it on YouTube and we're in trouble. Werewolves can no longer take their sons from their mothers and trust they'll never be caught. Nor can they ignore their daughters and trust that the girls can't track them down. A connected world means a new way of thinking. And as one of those kids taken from his mother, I'm glad to see those ways pass."

I opened my mouth, but he wasn't stopping, only pausing for breath, his tone still calm, with a conviction I don't know if I'd ever heard from him.

"I look at Reese," he said. "Raised by both his parents, and you couldn't hope to find a better-adjusted kid, in spite of what he's gone through. I look at Madison, and what she does for the Pack, and I know we're lucky to have her. Same as Vanessa, with her skills. And speaking of Vanessa, I might not have been looking for a mate, but I'm very happy to have had the option when I found one. So, yes, it's not your Pack.

It's better, and everyone else in it agrees, so if you want to do your crotchety old man thing, go find an old-school Pack that suits you better."

Malcolm snorted, turned on his heel and walked away.

"I just wasted my breath, didn't I?" Nick said.

"I thought it was good," Davis called to him. "It makes sense. Times change and we have to change with them. Like you said, it's a different world, with the Internet and everything. But it's hard on the old-timers. Hell, they're lucky if they know how to turn on a computer, let alone use it to research anything."

Malcolm shot a glare over his shoulder. Nick went to Davis and patted the young man's back. "You're okay, kid."

Davis gave a small smile. "For a Cain?"

"Not every Cain causes trouble," I said. "It's just the ones who do that we remember. And, Nick, it was a good speech."

"But, yeah," Clay said, "a waste of breath. Try hitting him next time. It might not work any better, but it feels good."

I shook my head, and watched Malcolm go. Then we returned to the bodies. ⌒

Fifteen

I DID CHANGE TO track the scents. I felt foolish for having reverted to human form. Admittedly, given Clay's disposition after the fight, I'd have wanted to Change back and talk to him, but if I'd given it more thought, the Alpha in me might have won out and delayed that talk. So I was, in a way, glad I'd been distracted, even if it meant a second Change. Clay Changed too—it's never as big a deal for him.

We'd searched for signs of a possible werewolf attacker at the site of Lonny and Curtis's deaths, but hadn't found a scent. Here we did, very plainly. Four humans and a werewolf tracking the Cains.

When the trail started, the four Cains stuck together. I could pick up Theo and Ford's scents, having met both before. The other two, presumably, were Nate and Carter. The Cains had walked into the desert and then paced around, as if waiting to meet their contact. The other men showed up, and that encounter ended in gunfire. We found shells along with blood drops that seemed to be Theo's. Warning shots, I'm guessing, to scatter the Cains. Except, being Cains, they didn't scatter, no more than Pack wolves would. At first they did split up. Someone stayed with Theo, who was wounded. But they'd regrouped, and we found that spot easily enough, because there was a human corpse to mark it—a body abandoned and scavenged in a patch of scrub brush.

From the scent trail, they'd seemed to go after another assailant, but Theo's injury was worsening, the blood trail heavier. They'd separated again. One of the grandsons—Nate or Carter—took Theo, and the other two Cains had found a place to Change. Their clothing was still there, along with one cell phone.

The two wolves had managed to wound another attacker. We found signs of a fight and the ground soaked with enough blood that I suspected the wounds had been fatal. The attack, however, must have been loud enough to bring the other three running. That's where the two Cains died. They'd taken down their prey and the rest of the party had heard it in time to make sure the wolves didn't escape alive.

By the process of deduction, one of our corpses was Ford

Cain, the werewolf who'd interrupted our honeymoon. The other, by my guess, was Nate. Davis had said Carter was "small for a Cain," which apparently meant not much bigger than Clay. The two bodies we'd found had been roughly equal in size.

That left Theo and Carter.

We followed their trail. So had the werewolf in that pack of hunters. He stuck close enough to it that he'd obviously changed to wolf form. Following Theo's trail had been easy. I could still see the blood, as well as the spots where his boots had dug in as he'd stumbled, Carter keeping him upright. Seeing the trail, I was sure they didn't have a chance. But there are only a handful of old werewolf families in the country, and while the Cains have survived partly by having a lot of sons, it's also because they knew a few things about werewolf survival.

We followed the trail up the side of a craggy hill. That obviously hadn't been easy for Theo—there were spots thick with scent, where he must have rested. But he'd made it up and then their trail vanished, as if they'd kept climbing into the sky. Or, you know, cut across the rocks and then jumped down.

I managed to follow their trail out onto the rock, but the werewolf tracking them had lost it. Down on the other side of the hill, I could find the werewolf and his cohorts' trails, as the werewolf paced back and forth, searching for the outgoing trail. He never found it. I did…leading from a deep, cave-like crevice in the rocks where the Cains had holed up, downwind, and waited for their pursuers to retreat.

The Cains' trail ended about a half-mile after that at an abandoned house. We turned off about a hundred feet away, Changed back behind some rocks and took our clothing from Nick. When we got out, Malcolm was there, having apparently been following at a distance, like the kid who doesn't want to be seen with his family but doesn't want to lose his ride home either.

"Uncle Theo's inside with Carter," Davis said. "I went downwind and caught their scents."

I nodded. "All right, so—"

"I was thinking…" Davis began.

"Don't," Clay said.

Davis shot him a scowl, but Nick said, "What Clay means is, don't interrupt. The Alpha is talking. Let her finish."

"Go ahead," I said.

"Sorry. I didn't mean to cut you off. I was just going to suggest that I go in there alone. I'll say that I tracked them here, and I'll get a feel for the situation."

"The situation is that we have four dead werewolves," I said. "I know Theo isn't going to be thrilled that you brought the Pack, and I understand this may cause you trouble, but we aren't messing around. We've already alerted your kin to take precautions. We haven't mentioned your involvement. So your option at this point is to come inside with us or stay out here, and we'll let on that we got an anonymous tip about Curtis and Lonny."

Davis squared his shoulders. "No, I'll go in. Otherwise, if they smell me and figure it out, it'll be even worse, hiding it from them." ⌒

Sixteen

I STOOD TO THE side of the biggest broken window and called, "Theo Cain? It's Elena Michaels."

A shuffling inside. Then a young man's voice whispered, "Did you hear that?"

"I'm not deaf, boy," Theo replied.

"I told you someone was behind this. Now we know who. The Pack."

"Yeah," Clay drawled. "We're so busy now, with the kids and all, that we've started contracting out our kills."

"Clayton..." Theo growled.

"Did you think she was here alone? Yeah, I know I'm not your favorite—"

"You killed my boy."

"That was a lotta years ago, and he killed my Pack mate."

"We know what happened to Nate and Ford," I said. "And we know you're badly injured. If we wanted to take you out, we wouldn't be announcing ourselves first. May we come inside and talk?"

Silence. Long enough that I was expecting a *Go to hell.* Finally, Theo said, "All right, but you gotta let yourself in. We're both hurt bad."

"Okay. We're coming inside."

I motioned to Nick. He fell in beside me. We went in the front door, paused to look around, and continued through to the back room where I could hear Theo's labored breathing. When we were close enough to see Theo propped against a wall, a figure charged from a side room...as Clay lunged and grabbed him back.

Clay wrenched Carter's arm behind his back and shoved him through ahead of us.

Theo sighed and waved at Nick. "*That* is not Clayton Danvers."

Carter scowled at Nick, as if this was his fault. "I heard he was a pretty boy. That's a pretty boy."

"Why thank you," Nick said.

Carter's scowl deepened. "It's supposed to be an insult."

Theo sighed. Again. Then he looked at Nick. "You look like your father, so I'm guessing you're Nick Sorrentino." He turned to Clay without waiting for Nick's reply. "If you want to continue this conversation, you'll let my grandson go."

"And if you want your grandson to stay alive and uninjured," Clay said, "you'll stop trying to trick us. You're not very good at it, Theodore."

"Fuck you."

"And on that note," I said, "we're here to help. Which may seem unlikely, but you aren't the first werewolves these guys have targeted. We have a problem that needs solving."

"Bullshit," Carter said. "You're behind this."

"No. There were two other werewolves killed by the same men. And…" I trailed off. This wasn't how anyone should find out about their kin being murdered, but I didn't see any easier way to do it. "It was Lonnie and Curtis Cain."

"What?" Carter's face screwed up. "Bullshit. There's no way—"

"They were murdered by the same people, in a similar fashion. We have reason to believe the Cain family is the target."

"Davis," Theo said, trying to straighten. "One of our boys was living with—"

"He's fine," I said.

"Yeah," Carter said. "Fine and in your custody—in that cell you guys keep in your basement. Where you killed my Uncle Zack. You really do think we're stupid, don't you? The

Pack has always wanted us gone. Now you've come up with this plan, hiring mercenaries or Cabal grunts to exterminate—"

"No," said a voice behind us. "They're here because I called them."

Davis walked in.

Carter spun on him. "You called the fucking Pack?" He turned to Theo. "See? This is exactly my point. You think going to college makes him smart. But there's college smarts and then there's real-life smarts, and when it comes to that, he's a fucking moron."

"He called us because his uncle and cousin were dead," I said, "and he couldn't get any of you on the phone. He was concerned, and he knows the Pack looks after problems like this. We have a werewolf teaming up with humans—presumably other supernaturals—to wipe out your family. Ignoring it would tell the world the Pack doesn't give a shit, and it's open season on werewolves. We're *all* werewolves."

"You called the fucking Pack?" Carter said to Davis again.

Nick sighed. "Pretty speech, Elena, but he listens about as well as this one." He hooked a thumb toward the hall behind me, and I glanced over to see Malcolm standing there. "Maybe they can form their own Pack."

I walked further into the room, so Malcolm wasn't looming behind me. He moved into the doorway. Theo looked over and blinked. Then blinked again.

"Yes, Theo, it's me."

"Malcolm?"

"Not any quicker on the draw than you were fifty years ago, I see."

Theo lunged. Which meant, in his condition, that he managed to push halfway up and falter toward Malcolm, before both Davis and I leaped in and held him back.

"Don't, Uncle Theo," Davis said. "You'll only make it worse."

"I don't care. Get that son of a bitch out of my sight." He turned to Clay. "You might have killed my Zack, and I will not forgive you for that. You knew he was weak and following a stronger mind, and you murdered him for it. But as angry as I still am about that, it does not compare to…" He snarled in Malcolm's direction. "That bastard. My boy was twelve. *Twelve.* Out visiting his uncle and cousin, and this son of a bitch and his posse slaughtered them in their sleep. For doing absolutely nothing."

"Except being mutts," Malcolm said. "That's a choice you all made, and back then, it was the price you paid for it."

"He was a little boy!"

"And little boys grow up—"

"Wait outside, Malcolm," I said. "Now."

I expected him to balk. To at least take his sweet time obeying. But he only turned and walked out.

"You let him back in the Pack?" Theo said. "And you expect me to believe you're here to help?"

"Letting him back in is part of helping," I said. "As fucked up as it might sound. He's under our control, and if he slips—if he kills *anyone* without my say-so—he's dead."

"Yeah," Carter said. "That makes perfect sense. It's not like you could control him by, you know, killing him now."

"That would violate Pack law. I can't hold him accountable for past crimes against outside werewolves because he is right— that's how things were done back then. They were sanctioned kills, as much as we might regret that today. Nor can I execute him for crimes against the Pack, because he hasn't committed any. Nor do we have any evidence of man-eating. The human deaths we can clearly pin on him are either associates who betrayed him or supernaturals who were hunting him."

"Who gives a fuck about your stupid rules?" Carter said.

"They do," Davis said softly. "That's what makes them the Pack."

Carter spun on him. "And now you're one of them?"

"Of course not. I'm a Cain. And I called them to help Cains." He bent beside Theo. "We need to get help for you."

"Really?" Carter said. "I thought we'd just hang out here for a few more days. It seems like a nice place. We aren't cowering in this dump while he dies, moron. I called for help before my phone died. Uncle Bart will be here any minute.

In the meantime, I hiked to town and got food, water and painkillers." He pointed to the stash in the corner. "I look after my family. Which is more than you did for Lonny and Curtis. You left them to die while you ran away and called the Pack. Typical."

"I wasn't there," Davis snarled. "I was on a date."

"Date?" Carter laughed. "Seriously? Last time we were at a bar together, I went home with both the girls. They'd rather share me than go with you."

Davis's face reddened and he lunged, but Nick caught him and pulled him back.

"Don't let him get to you," Nick said. "He's just being an ass. I don't think he knows how to be anything else."

"Yeah, pretty boy? I—"

"Enough," I said. "Theo? Please control your grandson or I'm going to ask him to step outside with Malcolm."

"Carter," Theo said.

"I'm not afraid of that old man," Carter muttered.

"You should be," Theo said. Then he looked from me to Clay. "I don't think she's really the Alpha, but I'll play along with the charade. So, Elena Michaels, tell me how you're going to save my family." ⌒

Seventeen

Y TALK WITH Theo was brief, mainly because the old man needed more than the bandages and painkillers Carter had swiped from a pharmacy. Nick fetched the rented SUV. Davis went with him. Carter may have phoned Theo's brother, Bart, but it didn't take two days to drive from just over the New Mexico border. Even Theo seemed to realize Bart wasn't coming "any second now," as Carter said.

We got Theo in the back of the SUV, leaving the rear seat down. I crawled in there, as did Davis, and we re-bandaged the old man's wounds, which started bleeding again during the transfer. Theo was in bad shape. Really bad. Two days without proper care hadn't helped.

As soon as he was settled, I was on the phone to Paige, asking for the nearest supernatural doctor who'd treat a werewolf. While our physiology isn't different from other supernaturals, their doctors often aren't comfortable dealing with us, even on our deathbeds. She promised to find someone, even if it meant using her leverage with the Cortez Cabal.

When I hung up, Davis caught my attention and mouthed "shock," casting a worried look at his great-uncle. I saw what he meant. The old man's face was paler than ever, his lips trembling, his eyes unfocused.

We'd brought the blankets from the house—more stolen goods, with the tags still hanging off them. We wrapped Theo up, and I kept him focused by asking him to verify the list of Cains that Davis had provided. That helped, and the shock seemed to pass, leaving him exhausted.

When we reached the end of the list, he mumbled that it was correct. Then he closed his eyes for about two seconds before he half opened them and said, weakly, "No. Derek. There's Derek."

"Okay," I said. "Who's—"

"Ask Carter," Theo mumbled. "Photo. Wallet. Need to warn him."

He drifted off. I looked up at Davis.

"Do you know a Derek Cain?"

"Uh…" He gave a helpless shrug. "No?"

"Carter?" I said, though I knew the kid had overheard from the back seat.

Carter kept facing forward and said, "Nope. I don't know a Derek."

"Did I hear him wrong? Maybe Eric?" I reached down to take out Theo's wallet.

"Wait!" Davis said. "Isn't Derek his grandson? Carter?"

"I know all Granddad's boys. There's no Derek."

"Maybe the name's wrong, but there is another grandson, right? Zachary's boy?"

"Zack Cain's son died years ago," I said. "In a challenge fight."

"See?" Carter said. "Even the Pack knows. Granddad's just confused. He's old and he's sick. Ignore him."

"God, you are such a—" Davis bit off the word and turned to me. "Uncle Theo isn't confused. There's another grandson. I remember them talking about him."

"Fucking fairy tale," Carter muttered.

"You *met* the guy. How can that be—?" Again he bit it off, shaking his head. He reached under Theo and took out the old man's wallet as he talked. "Zachary had another son. He just didn't know it. One of the Cabals was running genetic modification experiments, and they had a subject seduce Zack."

"Genetic modification?" Carter scoffed. "How does that even sound legit?"

"From a Cabal?" Nick called from the front seat. "Totally legit. And the part about Zack being seduced and not realizing he'd left a kid behind? Equally legit."

"So this kid claimed he was Zack's son," I said.

"Yeah, the key word there is *claimed*," Carter said. "He was just some werewolf brat trying to weasel into our family."

"No," Davis said as he fingered through Theo's wallet. "Some other werewolf sold the information to Uncle Theo."

"Sold him a load of bullshit, you mean."

Davis plucked out a photo and passed it over. The kid in the shot wasn't more than sixteen or seventeen. It looked like a surveillance photo, taken as the boy walked through the woods. He must have heard a sound because he'd glanced toward the camera. Scowled at it, more like.

There was no doubt the boy was a Cain. From his surroundings, he looked already bigger than Clay—taller and brawnier. He had shaggy dark hair and his cheeks bore both acne and scars, as if from a serious case that was starting to clear. Even after it cleared he wouldn't be... Well, like I said, the kid looked like a Cain. Of course, the scowl didn't help. There was something about his eyes that made me take a second look. He had nice eyes—bright green and sharp, with a keen edge of intelligence.

He wasn't alone in the picture. There was a girl, on his far side, holding his hand. When he'd heard—or sensed—someone, he'd turned, mostly blocking her, as if putting her behind him. She was tiny, with reddish blond hair, one blue eye peeking from behind his back as she leaned partly around him, her free hand on his arm as if to move him aside and see what had caught his attention.

I passed the photo up to Nick. "Um, yep. That's a Cain." He paused and lifted the photo. "But he's got a cute little girlfriend. So this is Zack's son?" He held out the photo for Clay, who was driving.

"Looks like it," Clay said. "He's what? Sixteen?"

"He was back when that was taken," Davis said. "He's older than me. Twenty, maybe twenty-one. Uncle Theo tried to get him back. Carter was there, regardless of what he says. Anyway, the guy wasn't exactly thrilled to be kidnapped, even if it was by his family. He already has one. Other supernaturals. Sorcerers. I think. Uncle Theo nabbed him, and his girlfriend helped him escape."

"This little thing?" Nick said with a laugh.

"Hey, she's a supernatural, too," Carter said.

"Yeah, a *necromancer*," Davis said. "Not exactly kick-ass powers."

"It wasn't her as much as him," Carter said. "He tricked us. He's smarter than college boy here. Way smarter."

Davis shook his head and turned to me. "According to the guy who sold Uncle Theo the information, Derek's a math and science whiz." He quirked a smile. "Obviously the genetic manipulation worked. But the point right now is warning him, and I have no idea how to do that. The last I heard from Uncle Theo, there was a rumor that one of the Cabals was looking after the kids from the experiment."

"Looking after?" Nick said. "I don't like the sounds of that."

"Uncle Theo wasn't happy about it, but he said... Well, I think he understood that Derek needed more than he had to offer. Uncle Theo said that whatever we think of the Cabals, they would recognize the value of a boy like Derek, and they'd treat him well. Except he's not a boy now, so I don't know if he'd still be with them or..."

"We'll look into it," I said. Which we would...if we couldn't resolve this case fast enough. This kid wouldn't be as easy to track down as his kin, and I had to trust that that meant those stalking the Cains wouldn't easily find him either. For now I couldn't waste the resources. Not unless we hit a dead end and the delay put Derek Cain in jeopardy. ⌒

Eighteen

WE WERE AT a motel. Everyone needed rest, and while Paige had tracked down a doctor, he was in Albuquerque. That was a five-hour drive, which was too much for Theo in his condition. So we were getting a house call, so to speak.

We rented separate rooms this time. Davis stayed with Theo, watching over him, which really didn't impress Carter. Obviously the kid had some jealousy issues, and he snarled and grumbled about Davis playing nursemaid, but that didn't mean he offered to stay and help either. He stalked off, muttering something about getting food.

"Good idea," Nick called after him. "Bring back enough for everyone."

Carter shot him the finger as he stumped down the road.

"That's a no, I take it?" Nick looked over at me. "Should I keep an eye on him?"

I shook my head, and Clay said, "By this point we don't fucking care if he gets shot and skinned."

Which wasn't exactly true. But we were a little sick of Carter Cain.

"Do you want me bunking down with Malcolm?" Nick asked.

"No," Malcolm said as he walked past. He dangled a key. "Got my own. Yes, even I can afford this dump."

"You're welcome to stay with us," I said to Nick.

"No," Clay said. "You're not."

"Believe me, I wasn't planning to take her up on that. I'm too tired to worry about ducking falling lamps. I'll get us separate rooms...at opposite ends of the motel." He started toward the office, then turned. "If I pick up food, you want some?"

"Dumb question," Clay said.

"Leave it outside the door and go?"

"Also...?"

"Dumb question?" Nick smiled, shook his head and continued on.

WE DID NOT break any motel furniture that day. There was sex, of course, but it was more of the same as earlier—the sweet and slow sex that's a lot rarer for us. We were tired and out of sorts, partly from Malcolm and partly from the fact that, yes, helping the Cains didn't exactly feel natural.

It was the right thing to do. Not ethically or morally right, but simply the right move for the Pack, to prove we were in control and capable of squashing threats to our kind, even if there'd been times we'd have been happy to see the whole Cain clan exterminated. And I think some of the discomfort arose from that, too. The Cains had been a royal pain in our ass for generations. It was easy to roll our eyes and joke about wanting them wiped out. As individuals, though? Yes, we could do without Carter Cain. Even Theo was no friend of ours. But if you joke about wiping out a family, you're including those like Davis, who seemed like a good kid, and Nate Cain, who by all accounts had been a decent guy.

But for the next couple of hours, Clay and I pushed all that aside, immersing ourselves in each other, making love and dozing, curled up together. We woke to Nick rapping at the door with pizza. We brought him in and left the door open for the others as we ate and talked. Then we video-called the kids. We were signing off when Davis raced into the room. He saw us in bed and his hands shot up, as if to cover his eyes.

"They're dressed," Nick said, laughing at the kid's horrified expression. "Well, they're decent anyway. If the door's open, it's safe to come in."

"Okay. Sorry. Just...have you guys seen Carter?"

Clay took another slice of pizza. "Nope, and we're happy to keep it that way for as long as possible."

"I know, I know. I warned you he was a dick. But the thing is that he came back about twenty minutes ago with food for Uncle Theo. None for me, of course, so I asked if he'd watch his grandfather while I did a takeout run. He was grumbling, and I was giving him shit, and then he saw something outside the window and said he'd do it in a minute."

"And never came back?" I guessed.

"Yeah, so I figured he was being a jerk, but he's not around. And the old guy—Malcolm—is gone, too."

We pulled on the rest of our clothing and hurried out. Nick had already checked the rooms and confirmed that both Malcolm and Carter were gone. I asked him to stay with Theo. First, though, he walked to the road with us.

We were outside the city, on a road that would have been rural ten years ago. Now it connected El Paso to a new housing development. I'm sure in another ten years, the motel would be replaced by a big-box store. Until then, it was on an otherwise undeveloped patch of land with what looked like commercial outcroppings on either side.

"You've got more motels and a truck stop down there," Nick said, pointing left. "Fast food and pizza to your right."

"In other words, two directions they might have gone," I said. "Which means the old stop-drop-and-sniff and hope no truckers run off the road wondering what the hell I'm doing."

"Yep." He patted my shoulder before walking away, calling back, "Enjoy."

"You could pretend to be tying your shoe," Davis said. "That's what I do."

"In a public place, I would. But after a few decades with this guy—" I nodded toward Clay "—I've learned not to give a shit. I'm serious about the truckers, though. One time I did this, I nearly got run over by an eighteen-wheeler, the guy trying to figure out why the blond chick was on her hands and knees at the side of the road."

I crouched and inhaled. Then I continued doing that—periodically stopping and getting as low to the ground as I could. The road was busy enough that a few people did slow. I wasn't alone, though, so they figured I was fine. Just weird.

I picked up Carter and Malcolm's trails heading left, but a few feet apart, meaning one was following the other.

"Do you think the old guy went after Carter?" Davis said.

"Malcolm," I said.

"Right, sorry."

"*Old guy* works for me," Clay said. "*Psychotic son of a bitch works, too.*"

Davis looked over to see if Clay was joking. When Clay shrugged, Davis turned to me. "Uncle Theo says he's dangerous. Is he? I mean, obviously he was, and I heard him and, uh..." He glanced at Clay. "Mr. Danvers..."

"Clay."

"Only his students call him Mr. Danvers," I said. "Well, technically, Doctor Danvers or Professor Danvers, but don't start doing that or he'll get used to it."

Clay rolled his eyes.

"Right," Davis said. "You're a college prof. Anthropology, isn't it? I took a course—" He shook that off. "Sorry, wrong time. Anyway, I was saying that I heard you two getting into it good in the desert, but I wasn't sure if you were going easy on him because he's old."

"He's old *and* he's dangerous," I said. "Clay wasn't going easy on him. You don't want to pick a fight with Malcolm. Ever. Not just because he's a good fighter, but because Clay isn't exaggerating when he said he's psychotic. Maybe not *clinically*, but he's done things that definitely qualify."

"But..." He snuck a look at Clay. "The Pack does crazy things sometimes, right? To show they mean business."

"Yes," I said. "And that's not Malcolm's excuse. He just likes it. No one else does."

A few minutes of silent walking. Then Davis cleared his throat. "Look, I want to apologize for something. Back when I met your son, I said some things…"

"I know," Clay said.

"I didn't tell him what you'd done to, uh, outside werewolves, and I wouldn't have. But I was…I was a bit of an ass." He exhaled. "No, I was a Carter-sized ass. I said I was going to tell him what kind of father he had, and that was just me being a complete jerk. I'd had a few drinks. Liquid courage. It didn't make me brave. Just a dick. I'd like to apologize for that. It was totally uncalled for."

"Logan was fine," Clay said. "Which is the only reason we're here, helping you."

"Okay. Well, I'm sorry. I really am. I'm usually not that guy. I was just trying to be tough, and the fact I was doing it with a little kid only proves I'm not." He shoved his hands into his pockets. "Back to, uh, Malcolm, though."

"Stay away," I said. "And tell your cousin to do the same, though I know he's not likely to listen."

"Do you think Malcolm went after him? He seems really pissed off about you guys helping us."

"Let's just follow this trail. We won't know what's going on until we get to the end of it." ⌒

Nineteen

AT THE END of Malcolm's trail, we found a truck stop restaurant. Carter's trail had separated from it back by the road.

"So they were just heading in the same direction," Davis said as we watched Malcolm through the window.

"Seems that way," I said. "Do you see any sign of Carter?"

Davis shook his head.

"All right," I said. "I'm going to backtrack and follow his trail a bit more. Clay will come with me. I'd like you to keep an eye on Malcolm." I waved to the nearest parked tractor-trailer. "Duck behind there. Don't let him catch you spying on him. If he does, run. With Malcolm, that isn't cowardice—it's common sense."

We left Davis heading toward the truck I'd suggested. As we returned to the road, I gave him a few shoulder checks. He did as I'd asked, tucking in behind the truck, hidden from sight.

I found Carter's trail again. It continued past the truck stop and turned on the far side of it, heading into an empty patch of scrubland.

"Where the hell was he...?" Clay began and then trailed off, his nose wrinkling as we caught the acrid scent of urine.

"And that answers your question." I picked my way carefully toward the smell. I didn't go far. Let's just say Carter was one of those mutts who pisses like he's a wolf marking territory. It was everywhere.

"Okay, so he diverted for this and then must have returned to the road. If Malcolm was stalking or luring him, this would have been the best spot to attack, and there's no scent of Malcolm here. False alarm."

We headed back toward the road. As soon as we passed the truck stop restaurant, I glanced over to where we'd left Davis, ready to wave for him to join us. The spot was empty.

"Goddamn it," I muttered. "Just when I was thinking he took direction well..."

We veered that way, walking along the front of the restaurant. I glanced through the window to see Malcolm's table...holding only empty dishes and a ten-dollar bill.

"Shit," I said, picking up speed. "No, no, no..."

I jogged around the side of the building, near the doors. As soon as I did, I picked up Davis's scent.

"Okay," I murmured. "Malcolm didn't catch Davis spying on him. The kid went in after him. When we *warned* him, in no uncertain terms—"

"His trail doesn't go inside," Clay said, straightening from a crouch. "He was heading around the building."

"Was Malcolm luring him?" It was a trick he'd played with Vanessa's agent, letting her think she was hunting him, only to get her into a deserted building and attack.

"I'm not smelling Malcolm," Clay said.

We headed around the back of the building, and I spotted Davis, creeping along a row of parked cars. When he stopped and crouched, I realized he was looking under the trailer. I followed the trajectory of his gaze and, sure enough, there was Malcolm, out for a stroll among the trucks.

"So," I murmured. "Do you think Malcom's just out stretching his legs after lunch?"

Clay snorted and we picked up the pace.

"I did tell Davis not to follow Malcolm, right?" I whispered.

"Yeah, darling. He's a Cain. A little brighter than average, but still a Cain. Better grab him before Malcolm does."

Davis stopped suddenly. I thought he'd heard us. He lifted his head to sample the air, but we were downwind.

Malcolm continued on. And Davis...

"What the hell is he doing?" I muttered.

The answer was obvious. I just couldn't believe what I was seeing. The kid had darted to the next truck and was climbing onto the trailer.

Malcolm was right on the other side, strolling along, knowing he'd picked up a tail and luring the boy in.

Davis picked his way carefully across the back of the trailer, hunched down so Malcolm wouldn't see his shadow. Then, when he reached the edge, he crouched and—

"Shit!" I said.

We broke into a run, tearing across the parking lot. It was too late to stop Davis. He'd already jumped. The only thing I could hope was that Malcolm wouldn't snap the kid's neck the second he landed. That he'd toy with him a little, as he usually did.

It sounded as if that was exactly what he was doing. I heard the thud of Davis hitting the ground. Heard a grunt and a thud and a hiss of pain. Then, "Back the fuck off!"

That was Davis, and I slowed, just a little, thinking I must have heard wrong. Did Davis honestly expect Malcolm to back off when Davis's ambush failed?

Still running, we rounded the line of trucks.

"I said back the fuck off!" Davis snarled. "I've got this."

"No, boy, I've got this," Malcolm said. "Now you back off or—"

That's when they heard our pounding footfalls, and we saw them. *Three* of them. Davis had Carter pinned to the side of a truck while Malcolm advanced on them.

"He's right, Malcolm," I called. "Back off."

I slowed to a fast march. Carter struggled under his cousin's grip, but Davis outweighed him enough to keep him pinned.

"The boy tried to get the jump on me," Malcolm said.

"Carter, you mean," Clay said. "Davis was stopping him."

Malcolm snorted. "No, he was getting in the way."

Davis shot him a glare. "You're welcome, *old man*."

Another snort as Malcolm rolled his eyes. I walked to Carter and plucked a knife from his hand.

"I think you were in a little more danger than you figured," I said, waving the knife at Malcolm. "Someone doesn't play by the rules."

"Not when I'm trying to take down a fucking psycho," Carter said. "Maybe if you had the balls... Oh, wait."

"You could have cut him," I said. "You might even have cut him badly. But you wouldn't have killed him. It would've been your body lying on the ground with a knife through it. Then he'd have dumped you in the scrub over there, and even your kin would have figured you'd just gotten pissy and left."

I turned to Davis. "I'm guessing you spotted Carter going after him."

"I saw him go around the back of the building. I followed to find out why. Then I saw Malcolm."

"Who did not just happen to exit out the back door and stroll through the empty parking lot. Carter? Here's a hunting tip. If your prey decides to mosey into a conveniently dark or deserted spot, it's not Fate smiling on you. You've been made." I threw the knife under the truck. "Now let's get you back to your grandfather and see what he thinks of this little stunt."

"What?" Malcolm said. "He tried to murder a Pack member, and you're turning him over to his grandfather?"

"If we executed every werewolf who wanted you dead, there wouldn't be anyone left. Being part of my Pack means you're entitled to our protection. It does not mean you're entitled to our vengeance, especially after you egged him on by coming out here."

I waved for Davis to keep hold of Carter as we headed back to the motel.

Twenty

THEO CAIN WAS furious. Well, outwardly furious, for his grandson's sake and for ours. Carter had done a very stupid and nearly suicidal thing, and Theo made sure he understood that. But he also, I suspect, was proud of his grandson. Proud that he'd made the effort to avenge his family. And not quite so pleased with Davis for stopping him.

The doctor arrived after that. He patched Theo up and then took me aside.

"I've never treated a werewolf," he said, in a tone that suggested he could have lived his life without that particular experience. "I know your race is rumored to have accelerated healing abilities."

"We do."

"Then he might pull through. But I doubt it."

And that was all we got. The rather cold assessment that Theodore Cain's injuries were fatal. They'd done serious damage internally, and it was too late to repair that. The best we could do was keep him comfortable and feed him a steady diet of painkillers.

Despite the doctor's obvious distaste for werewolves, I was sure he'd done all he could. Other supernaturals may not like us, but they fear us enough not to screw us over, especially when the only satisfaction would be prodding an already old werewolf closer to his grave.

The doctor was on his way out when Vanessa called. She had a line on "the Russian" that Marsh had given us, and it was time for the interrogation, which she knew better than to conduct alone.

I'd join her. Davis and Carter would stay here, in the motel, to look after Theo. As for Clay, Nick and Malcolm, I had another task for them. Bart Cain never had shown up and further attempts to contact him had failed. Which made me worry that we had another Cain to add to the body count. The guys would go investigate while Vanessa and I chatted to this Russian.

I didn't have far to go to meet up with Vanessa. With cyber-help from her team, she'd tracked the Russian to El Paso. Which was obviously no coincidence. He was involved with the Cain massacre, and they were still hoping to capture

Theo and Carter. I wasn't overly concerned they'd find them. I'd confiscated Davis and Carter's phones and all their credit and debit cards and left them with a wad of cash for food— and orders to stick with takeout.

I met Vanessa at the airport. We made a pit stop for lunch to discuss details. By the time we'd ordered our meals, Vanessa had finished telling me everything she knew about the guy we were supposed to meet, which boiled down to "not a hell of a lot."

His name wasn't in their databases, which made sense if he was an immigrant. They'd tracked credit card use under that name, which didn't tell us more than where he liked to eat. It did show that he'd been in the States for a few months. Moving around, staying in hotels.

"Possibly a mercenary," Vanessa said. "He has money— he's staying in good hotels and eating at expensive restaurants. And he's moving around enough to suggest he doesn't have a steady job."

I looked at the list of cities. Something about them looked familiar, but I couldn't place it.

Vanessa hadn't been able to locate a cell phone, which supported her mercenary theory. Presumably he had one, but it would be a burner, leaving no record. In other words, he was making no serious effort to hide his whereabouts, but did make damned sure no one knew who he was chatting with.

Lunch arrived and we were quiet for a couple of minutes as we dug in. She blurted, "Nick asked me to move in with him." She caught my expression and said, "He didn't mention it, I see."

"He wouldn't until he was sure the answer was yes. Or, if it's no, he'd get my advice on how to change that."

She nodded. "My niece graduates in a couple of months and my apartment lease is up shortly after that. So he's suggesting we move in together."

"At the estate?"

She pushed pasta around on her plate. "That's up to me. I can move in with him or we can get our own place. Adding another dilemma to the pile."

"Which starts with…?"

"Moving in with someone else at all. I'm forty years old, and I've only come close to moving in with a guy once. I valued my independence more than I valued living with a lover. Nick is different."

"So you want to move in with him?"

"Hell, yes. Without question. Which scares the shit out of me. I don't like to…"

"…take a risk," I finish for her. "I know you've been cautious with Nick. He's never been a model of monogamy. He hasn't ever cheated, though, I can tell you that much."

"Only because—before me—he never had a monogamous relationship last long enough. It's one thing if we're just dating and he decides this isn't what he wants. Moving in together takes it to a whole other level."

"Well, considering that I've never known Nick to date anyone exclusively for more than a few months and you guys have passed the two-year mark, I'd say that's about as good a test run as you can expect. The problem is that for you, moving in says, 'This is it.' You're acknowledging how you feel and that you want to share your life with someone for as long as you can."

"Yep."

"And if you say no, he's going to think you aren't as committed as he is, and he might back off."

"Yep."

"Then don't play games. You never have before. Nothing's guaranteed, but with Nick, you are a thousand times closer to it than any other woman has ever been."

She exhaled. "I know, and I hate needing the reassurance."

"Given who we're talking about, I don't blame you. Now, the question of residences…"

"He says the boys and Antonio would be fine without him. Which is bullshit. Yes, they'd be *fine*, but no one is going to be happier if Nick's not there—including Nick. It's his home."

"Which is the problem. It's *his* home. It isn't that you don't want to move in. It's that you feel you shouldn't. It's the

Sorrentino estate, and it's Pack territory. You're fine with it. But will they be fine with having *you* there?"

She managed a weak smile. "Nailed it. I understand the territorial issue, but it's more than that. I'm an interloper in every way. It's only been in the last year that I've started spending weekends. We've just moved past the point where they feel the need to get fully dressed before grabbing coffee in the morning."

"Hey, that's progress."

"It is. They *seem* fine with me. But there's a difference between having me spend every other weekend and having me move my stuff into their closets."

"I understand where you're coming from. Only female werewolf, remember? These were guys who had never—*never*—lived under the same roof with a woman, even a mother. At least Reese and Noah have done that. They'll adjust."

She nodded. "I don't want to take Nick away from his home. I really, really don't. If it comes to that, we can't move in together."

"Then tell him so. Tell him you'll give it a shot and if it doesn't work, you'll get a place in New York, and he can divide his time. He'll be happy with that."

"I hope so." ⌒

Twenty-one

SOMETIMES, EVENTS CONVERGE in a way that makes you want to slap yourself silly for not seeing the obvious connection. Except the connection wasn't obvious at all—you just expect too much of yourself. I've been told that about myself before, but I never really believed it until I started seeing Logan pushing himself so hard and then beating himself up for making a mistake, and I want to throw up my hands and say, "You're *nine*, baby." I listen to him fretting about things he can't be expected to control, listen to him taking the blame for things that aren't really his fault, and I see myself, and I know that I have to stop doing that because *this* is my fault. He's my son. He emulates me, the good and the bad.

So then I beat myself up for making him that way. Which kinda defeats the epiphany that I have to stop expecting too much of myself.

Here, then, as we traveled to see "the Russian," I experienced another of those head-slapping moments. Those why-the-hell-didn't-I-see-that bouts of self-recrimination. And I wasn't the only one.

One reason we'd stopped for lunch—besides the fact that I'm a werewolf and really like my meals on time—is that we didn't know exactly where to find the Russian. We had a hotel address, but it was unlikely he was just hanging out there at midday. From his credit card transactions, we knew he liked to eat out, which didn't mean grabbing a burger at McDonald's—though he did have plenty of fast food charges, as between-meal snacks. For meals, though, as Vanessa had said, he dined well, in the kinds of places that don't have takeout.

So while we ate an early lunch, we'd been waiting for Vanessa's colleagues to get a ping on his lunch bill. The call came just as we were leaving our restaurant, which happened to be—not by coincidence—in the same district where he liked to take his meals. He was only a few blocks over. As we walked, Vanessa talked to her operative. Then she said, "No, that's not surprising. I suspect Mr. Marsh's ear for accents is about as good as his eye for fine movie scripts. I didn't think the name sounded Russian. What is he, then?"

There was a pause. A long one, and when I looked over, Vanessa was wincing.

"You're sure of that?" she said. Then, "Yes, I know. It's not proof positive, but…shit. Look, I'm going to send you another name. It might be a second alias. Can you check it out? Thanks."

"What's up?" I said as she texted the name.

"I'm a moron, that's what." She finished and then pulled up a note on her phone and listed off three cities.

"That's where the Russian has been," I said.

"Our Russian isn't Russian. He's Albanian."

"Alban…" I trailed off and as I did, a scent wafted over, just the faintest smell, but unmistakable to my nose. It was the scent of one of the men who'd killed the Cains.

The werewolf.

"Ruçi," I said. "The Albanian werewolf you and Nick have been tracking."

"Yep. *Goddamn* it. Here I was thinking, 'Huh, why do those cities sound familiar?'"

She gave a sharp shake of her head, and I said, "I was thinking the same, and also, 'Huh, this guy really likes to eat, all those restaurant meals with takeout in between.'" I caught the scent again. "But, as much fun as it is to beat ourselves up for not seeing the connection sooner, from the smell of things, he's on the move and not far away. We'd better catch up before he reaches his car. Are you ready for that?"

She nodded and pulled something from her jacket. "All set." ⌒

Twenty-two

WE BROKE INTO a run, ignoring the odd looks from passersby. We weren't running fast enough for anyone to think we were being pursued and try to "help," and that's all that mattered. We got odd looks but no interference.

I followed the mutt's scent on the breeze. A moment later I caught a glimpse of the man from Nick's file turning into a parking lot ahead. We cut down a side street and through to the lot, tucked behind buildings. Then I fell back, staying out of sight and downwind.

Vanessa picked up her pace. We knew what kind of car the guy was driving. We even knew the license plate, from Vanessa's team accessing the rental company's records. She headed straight to his vehicle and got there about ten paces before he did. She took out a key fob and pressed it, and then frowned and peered into the car just as the mutt stepped up beside her.

She started in surprise, and then gave a small laugh. "Uh, let me guess. Your car?"

"It is."

"Well, that's a little embarrassing. Apparently, I need to pay attention to more than the color when I rent a vehicle."

She smiled, and he checked her out in a deliberately slow once-over. The mutt—Ruçi—looked in his mid-thirties. Blond hair, as well-built as the average werewolf, with that slightly smarmy demeanor that says he knows he's an attractive guy. Vanessa is also very attractive—elegant and perfectly dressed, with long curling dark hair, arrestingly strong features and a body that belongs on a forties pinup model. She gives off an aura of sophistication and confidence that makes most men steer clear, but the mutt kept checking her out, and there was a glint in his eyes that made my hackles rise. He was a werewolf looking at an intimidating woman and not thinking, "I like that," but, "I could break her."

I resisted the urge to call Vanessa back. She said something else to him that I didn't catch, but from her tone, it was just a moment of friendly conversation. Then she headed off, scouring the lot for "her" rental car. Ruçi gave her one last lingering look, and then got into his vehicle and drove off.

We tailed Ruçi's car. That was easy enough, given that Vanessa had stuck a tracker on it. I hoped he'd lead us to the rest of his hunter pack. Instead, he returned to his hotel.

I had to let Vanessa take it from there. He would recognize her scent from the encounter, but it wouldn't trigger alarm bells the way mine would. She kept in touch with me via texts, saying he didn't seem to have noticed her follow him inside. She watched the elevator climb and then hightailed it up the stairs. Fortunately, he'd only gone to the third floor and she made it out of the stairwell in time to see which doorway he walked through.

I followed her up and stood watch in the hall as she rapped on his door.

"Hello," she said when he answered. "Remember me? Seems we're staying at the same place. I don't mean to be forward, but I was wondering if you'd like to come down to the lounge for a drink."

Given a few moments, I'm sure he'd have realized the unlikelihood of this coincidence. But as she spoke, I'd crept along the wall until I was a few feet from his open door.

"On second thought," Vanessa said, "maybe I'll just come inside and get a drink from the minibar." She pulled her gun and kicked him back, and before he could recover, I was in the room, launching myself at him and sending him flying into the wall.

Vanessa came in and shut the door. She stood there as we fought, rolling on the floor, grappling for the upper hand.

"I could let you two finish," she said. "I know you guys are all about the dominance thing, but as you can tell, Mr. Ruçi, Elena's not the submissive type. Now that you realize she's a serious contender, let's save the bumps and bruises, and declare her the winner."

Ruçi snarled up at her. Which was exactly the distraction I needed to land a solid uppercut. He flew back. I pinned him.

"Well, that worked," Vanessa said. "Of course, considering that I have a gun, it's not like you can escape anyway. But now we can skip the asking-nicely part. I'm guessing you know who she is?"

"The Danvers bitch," he said in a thick accent.

"Technically, yes," she said. "Can't fault you for that word with a female werewolf, though she usually goes by Michaels. Now get up and let's have a seat."

I grabbed him, wrenching his arm back, and propelled him into the sitting room part of the suite.

"Or we can do that," Vanessa said.

"The asking-nicely thing really doesn't work with werewolves."

She grinned. "Depends on the werewolf."

I shoved Ruçi onto the armchair and said, "Sit and stay."

He scowled up at me and unleashed a torrent of Albanian, undoubtedly calling me a whole lot worse than bitch.

"Get it out of your system," Vanessa said. "It's not like we understand you anyway."

"Then maybe you will understand this," he said. "You are making a very big mistake."

"I get that one a lot." Vanessa moved closer, her gun trained on him. "Now, if you're done cursing your bad luck, Elena wishes to speak to you."

I didn't give him time to respond. "We know you've been assisting other supernaturals in killing members of the Cain family. Why?"

Ruçi shrugged. "I do not ask details. I follow my instructions."

"Did your Alpha set this up?"

"I do not have an Alpha." He sneered as he said it. "No one rules over me."

"Then you wouldn't take a job without asking for details, would you? No werewolf would, for anyone but an Alpha."

"I can make exceptions if I am properly compensated. I am not like you American wolves. My family has worked with Cabals in Europe for many generations. It is a good relationship."

"European Cabals wouldn't dare hunt supernaturals on American Cabal territory, no more than we'd hunt werewolves on another Pack's territory. Which means this isn't a Cabal job. You aren't going to do it without knowing details. They're hiring you as a specialized mercenary, not a dumb thug."

"I wouldn't be too sure about that," Vanessa said. "He was too busy checking out my boobs to notice I put a tracker on his car. If one of my field agents screwed up that badly, she'd be on desk duty for a year."

Ruçi scowled. "My skills are indeed specialized. They do not include technology gadgets."

"Well, they should," Vanessa said. "But okay, so you're not a dumb thug, yet you allowed someone to hire you with nothing more than a laundry list of instructions. Go here. Do this. Kill him. Now go back to your hotel and wait until we need you."

His face darkened. "It is not like that."

"I'm sure it's not," I said. "Because you aren't going to hunt werewolves on American Pack territory without a damned good reason, in addition to that good paycheck."

"Why am I hunting these Cains? Because they deserve it. Because *they* are the thugs."

"Maybe, but they've been that for hundreds of years and no one's tried to wipe them out yet. What did they do, specifically?"

"It is such a little thing that I can understand why you did not bother to punish them for it. After all, it was only a girl. Eighteen years old. Kidnapped and held in a cabin. Raped for

days. Murdered and then eaten." He met my gaze. "A small thing, no?"

I was sure my expression said otherwise, as much as I hated to give him that satisfaction. He smiled and said, "So perhaps you would agree that they deserve it? That I am not the monster here? Or is this how you allow American werewolves to behave?"

"Who hired you?" I asked.

"The girl's father. He wants to cover a wall in their hides. I can understand. I have a daughter. She is with her mother, of course, but I am still fond of her. I would skin any werewolf who did such a thing." He tilted his head. "I hear you have a daughter, Ms. Danvers. What would you do?"

"So the girl's father claims—"

"He does not 'claim.' He directed me to her grave, where I could smell the Cains and dig and see the condition of her corpse." He turned to Vanessa. "I am *not* a dumb thug, as you put it. I know how to conduct my business."

"Okay," I said. "But how the hell would *he* have found her grave?"

"He is a necromancer. When his daughter died, she did not pass over immediately. Her spirit found him and told him. After she watched the Cains devour her dead body."

I struggled not to react to what he was telling me. Not to think of the horror of what that girl had gone through, and the truth that, hell, yes, I'd have wanted the same fate to befall anyone who did that to Kate.

No, I'd have done it myself.

"That's why you castrated the corpses," I said. "Her father doesn't just want the hides."

"I did not personally do either," he said. "But yes, that is why it was done. He wanted them to be alive for both but..." He shrugged. "That is not possible, to keep a person alive during such a physical shock." He pursed his lips and looked at me. "Perhaps I should have spoken to your mate. I hear he has experience with similar procedures."

I didn't respond, and he smirked. He thought he'd rendered me speechless with the memory of what Clay had done. That hadn't bothered me in years. I don't like to imagine it, but I know why he did it and that it wasn't something he enjoyed.

What stopped me now was thinking about what the father of that girl wanted done. Keeping the Cains alive while skinning and castrating them. My gut screamed that it went too far, that I could never imagine sadism like that... and then was mentally silenced by the part of me that said, *Even if it was Kate?*

I didn't want to think about that. I have been placed in situations that have made me consider the death of my children more than any mother should need to. How terrible would my vengeance be, whether it was Clay or Kate or Logan?

How far would I go? How dark would I go? These are things I
don't want to consider, for my own sanity.

Vanessa saved me from a response by saying, "But you
didn't castrate *all* the corpses. Meaning this wasn't a gang rape
and murder by the whole Cain clan."

Yes, of course. Only Curtis's corpse had been castrated in
the forest, and Nate and Ford's bodies had been in too poor
a condition to see what had been done to them. And while I
suppose it would be possible—if horrifying to contemplate—
that an entire clan could hold a girl captive and rape her,
I could not imagine Theo allowing that. Couldn't imagine
Davis doing it. Nate, from what I'd heard, wouldn't have
taken part either.

"It was Curtis and Ford, wasn't it?" I said.

I expected Ruçi to sneer that he didn't bother with names,
but he was a professional. He knew damned well who his
primary targets were.

"Curtis, Ford and the boy," he said.

The boy? Carter's name sprang to my lips, but I pushed it
back. I had to be sure. Instead, I said, "Davis?"

"No. The older one. The better-looking one. Carter."

I tried not to exhale. Ruçi went on, "The people I am
working with are not convinced the other boy is innocent,
though. He is young, and he was living with Curtis, and they
believe the girl may have been mistaken when she identified

only three. The Cains have a similar look. It would be easy
to miss one. They told our employer this, and he has said we
cannot take any chances. He wants Davis's hide and his…
parts."

"And the others?" Vanessa said. "Lonny Cain, Nate
Cain… They weren't involved, yet you murdered and skinned
them, too."

"As I said, I did not participate in that. I only hunted. But
I take your point. My client's hunger for revenge is not limited
to those who attacked his daughter. He blames their kin, for
allowing them to grow up in such a way."

"So he wants the entire *family* wiped out?" I said.

"No. The three the girl identified. Plus the other three.
The old man, Theodore. The father, Lonny. The boy, Davis.
And any kin who are with them at the time. We will be paid
for all the hides."

Paid for all the hides. He said it so calmly that I couldn't cut
Ruçi any slack for taking this job. He might pretend he was
helping a grieving father find justice, but this wasn't justice. It
was a massacre, driven by blind rage.

"I want to know—" I began.

The *ding* of a typewriter return stopped me short, and
it took a moment to realize it was Ruçi's phone. When I
reached to take it from his pocket, his hands shot up,
knocking mine away.

"I am answering your questions," he said. "You will respect my privacy."

"Yeah, no, that's not how it works," Vanessa said. "Not when the only reason you're talking is because you're caught between a loaded gun and a pissed-off werewolf."

I reached for his pocket again. This time, when he caught my wrist, Vanessa grabbed his arm with her free hand. He looked at it and let out a laugh.

"Is that supposed to stop me?" he said.

"No, this is." She squeezed his arm and he yowled as her fingers burned him. He also released my hand—fast. I tugged out the phone and backed away while Vanessa released him and put the gun to his temple instead.

"I thought you said you had experience working with other supernaturals," she said. "You should know a gun wouldn't be my only weapon. I just prefer the one that doesn't require actually touching assholes like you."

He snarled under his breath. I checked the phone. A text had just come in, and the moment I read it, my head snapped up and Vanessa said, "And that look means we're cutting this conversation short. Now put your hands behind your back so Elena can make sure you stay put. And don't worry, these handcuff strips are werewolf-proof." She winked at me. "Tried and tested." ⌒

Twenty-three

HE TEXT THAT had come in on Ruçi's phone was only two words.

Targets acquired.

A second followed moments later, with the address of the motel where we'd left the Cains.

As we raced down the stairwell, I realized that in taking away the Cains' phones, we'd also eliminated any method of contact.

"It's a motel," Vanessa said as we jogged to the car. "It has a room phone."

"Which they're sure as hell not going to answer."

"Don't worry. I'm on it."

She made a call as I climbed into the driver's seat of the rental and roared out of the parking lot, my phone in hand, because driving safety wasn't really a major concern right now.

I got hold of Clay right away. He was already halfway back to El Paso. He'd left me a message, but I hadn't paused in my mad flight down the stairs to retrieve it.

"We found Bart Cain alive and well," Clay said after I told him the problem. I'd say he hit the gas when he heard it, but Clay treats speed limits as suggestions…for other people. Which meant he only continued as fast as he was already going, while talking to me.

"Or he was 'well' when we found him," he said, "but he really didn't want to talk to me, so he's a little worse for wear now. But still alive."

"Good."

"Yeah, so apparently, he forgot to go get Theo."

"Forgot a life-or-death call for help from his *brother?*"

"We are talking about Cains here. Seems Bart was dead-drunk when Carter called. He got in his car, drove out the driveway and missed that turn at the end. You know, the one that takes you onto the road."

"Uh-huh."

"He went through the ditch, hit a fence and, naturally, wasn't wearing a seatbelt."

"Naturally."

"He flew out the windshield. Did more damage to the car than to himself, probably because he was so damned drunk. Anyway, he hit his head, and when he woke up, he had no idea why he'd been in the car in the first place."

"Uh-huh."

"Also? His cell phone went out the windshield with him, and he hasn't found it yet, so our calls were going to the neighbor's cows."

"Helpful."

"This is why I love chasing Cains, darling. It's always entertaining. Point is that Bart's fine—except for the black eye and broken wrist I gave him. And I should be at the motel in less than an hour, which isn't going to help you much, but I'm guessing you're a whole lot closer."

"About fifteen miles out."

"And those guys who sent the text are going to wait for their werewolf tracker before they go after the Cains. Since you've left him incapacitated, you should be fine."

"I also texted his cohorts back, saying he got the message and will be there shortly."

"Perfect." A moment's pause. "And if there's any problem at the motel, you know who to focus on saving. Not the bastard who killed that girl. And not an old man who won't last the night."

"I know."

"'Course you do. But once you get there, if trouble breaks out, you're going to try to save them all. Not that Carter deserves it, but he's under your protection. So you'll want to save him and then…well, you know what you've got to do then."

"Order you to kill him for what he did."

"Which I'm fine doing, but given the choice between letting these guys execute him and the trouble that comes with doing it ourselves, especially in front of a decent kid who thinks the Pack isn't so bad after all?"

"I'll focus on Davis."

Vanessa got off her call a few moments after I ended mine.

"Well, I know how they found them," she said. "They made a phone call."

"What?" I glanced over. "No. I confiscated their cell phones *and* I disabled outgoing calls on their room phone."

"Carter took twenty dollars of what you gave them and went to the front office. The manager says he was calling New Mexico."

"Phoning Bart," I said. "That idiot."

"Oh, Carter probably thought he was being clever. He wasn't making a call from any number that could be traced to *them*."

"They just made one to a number that their pursuers must have been tracking."

"Presumably. I had the manager place a call to their room. They weren't picking up. So he went down and knocked. He can hear the TV on, but they aren't answering. I asked him to shove a note under the door. I think he figured I was joking. I promised him a hundred bucks if he does it. I still don't know if he will. But it seems they're fine. Just hunkered down with the telly blaring."

We arrived at the motel twenty-five minutes later. We'd have been sooner if I could have just driven into the parking lot, but I presumed our targets had the place staked out.

I parked a few doors down. Then we cut around the back of the neighboring buildings, through a strip of empty land that brought us to the rear of the motel. It was then that I realized, as nice as the desert was for running, it was a shitty landscape for subterfuge. Far too open, leaving us creeping through though the ruins of some long-demolished building as we drew closer to the motel.

The open land, though, meant I could see at a sweep that no one was staking the place out from this angle. We were darting along the motel's rear wall—aiming for the Cains' back window—when the sound of a raised voice stopped me.

It came from the direction of the manager's office.

The supernaturals chasing the Cains knew the motel address but not the room number. Without their werewolf tracker, if they wanted to launch their attack, they'd need to get that room number from the front office.

I motioned to Vanessa, and we changed direction, creeping along the side of the motel. Then Vanessa walked out and hailed a man who was storming away from the office, still cursing. I stayed in place, listening and waiting.

"Hey," she said. "I heard shouting. Any problems I should know about before I check in? No bedbugs, I hope."

"The problem will be checking in," the man grumbled. "There's no sign of the damned manager. He's locked in his back room with the radio blasting a baseball game. I tried knocking. I tried yelling. Nothing. We just got back to our room, and it stinks so bad my wife threw up."

"Ouch. Is she okay?"

"She's over there getting fresh air and hoping we don't need to make a trip to the emergency ward. Not how we planned to spend our vacation."

"I don't blame you. Guess I'm finding another motel, then."

"You and me both," he muttered, then said, "Good luck," before stomping off across the parking lot.

Vanessa came back to me. "He's legit. I can see his wife, and she's definitely looking a little green."

"Not liking the sound of that 'bad smell.' Or the manager locked in his back room with the radio blasting."

"Me neither. But there are only a few cars in the lot, all empty. No obvious signs of a stakeout."

"Let's take a look in the office." ⌒

Twenty-four

VANESSA PICKED THE lock on the manager's door. Even from outside I could tell what we'd find.

The man had complained of a "bad smell" that made his wife throw up. I'm guessing they must have had the room next to the manager's and she also must have both an excellent sense of smell and a very weak stomach. Or maybe just an excellent sense of smell and a normal human stomach, one that hadn't spent nearly as much time around dead bodies as mine.

Yes, the manager was dead. Shot in the head, presumably while he sat at his desk, the killer then dumping his body in the back room, turning up the radio, locking the door and cleaning the front room just well enough that a random passerby wouldn't see blood.

As soon as I heard about the radio blaring, I'd thought of the TV blasting in the Cains' room. But the sequence of events was wrong. If the killers shot the manager *after* getting the room number, they couldn't have killed the Cains and jacked up their TV to cover it, not if the manager had been alive to hear the TV.

That slowed me down enough to pop off a quick text to Nick. He replied that they were less than ten minutes away. I told him to drive right into the motel lot. With a dead body in the manager's office, we didn't want to be caught "sneaking" around. And with five of us, I wasn't nearly as worried about being ambushed by the killers.

Vanessa and I still scoped out the lot and surrounding area as we left the office. Just those same few cars, all empty. The man and his wife had left.

We hurried to the Cains' room. That's when I caught the smell, and I realized it wasn't a hyper-sensitive nose—or stomach—that made the man's wife vomit. It hadn't been the smell of blood at all. The odor was chemical.

"Gas," Vanessa said. "These guys are pros. They broke into the next room and pumped chemicals through into the Cains' room."

"Knock them out and then break in and kill them. The only way to do it without raising the alarm."

Just then, Clay's vehicle whipped into the lot. He parked on the other side and walked over to us as fast as he could without breaking into a run. Nick was out of the car seconds later, long strides catching up in a few steps. I motioned for them both to stay where they were and keep a watch—Clay surveying the road and Nick making sure no one peeked out from another room.

"Where's Malcolm?" Vanessa asked.

Died fighting Bart Cain would be an excellent answer. Sadly, I could see him over the rear headrests. "He's there—just not hurrying to get out and help."

She shook her head, and I covered her while she reached for the Cains' room door with one gloved hand. The knob turned easily.

I swung in first. She covered me with the gun. As soon as that door closed, we both had our shirts pulled up over our mouths and noses so we could breathe.

Theo Cain lay on the floor, his eyes open. The gas had been too much for him. His body was sideways, arms over his head, as if the boys had tried to drag him, but it was too late.

We checked the bathroom. Empty…with an open window. Carter and Davis had gone out that way. I was guessing their attackers hadn't had time to add reinforcements since losing one of their number in the desert. That meant that without Ruçi, there would only be two of them. Had they only bothered to cover the front door?

"No," Vanessa said. "That would be amateur hour. My guess? Without Ruçi here to advise them, they underestimated the amount of gas they needed."

They'd jumped the gun, gassing them before their werewolf arrived, which meant they'd pumped through enough to sedate humans. And enough to kill one old man on his deathbed. But not enough to knock out two healthy young werewolves. The boys had realized they were being gassed, gotten that window open, tried to save Theo and then escaped while their attackers waited for the gas to drop them flat.

Those attackers wouldn't have waited long, though. And as soon as they figured out the boys had run, they'd have given chase, out into the desert behind the motel.

Malcolm joined us for the hunt. I didn't give him a choice. I also made him Change forms.

"Because she told you to," Clay said when Malcolm asked why.

"Or because there are men with guns looking to shoot dark-haired wolves," Malcolm said.

"I need someone to Change to track," I said. "But if we meet up with these guys we need to be able to talk them down. You aren't that good at talking."

"And he is?" Malcolm motioned at Clay.

"Shut the fuck up and Change forms *now*," Clay said. "Is that good enough conversational skills for you?"

"You are going to Change, Malcolm," I said. "Nick will track with you. Vanessa will cover you with her gun. Clay and I will track separately. Nick, if you find the boys, get them the hell out. If you find their hunters, take them down if you can and take them out if you can't."

Clay and I set off. As Vanessa and I had discovered earlier, the motel backed onto what looked like the demolished remains of other buildings, set far enough away from the highway that no one had bothered to clear the ruins. I could pick up traces of scent—both the boys and their pursuers—but the ruins weren't extensive enough to provide a decent hiding place. Carter and Davis had cut through them and then split up.

Without Ruçi for tracking, the hired guns had been all over the area, crisscrossing the ruins, trying to find the boys by sight or sound. But Carter and Davis must have gotten enough of a head start to not leave much for their pursuers to go on, and while the mercenaries' trails went everywhere, the boys had cut straight through.

We followed Davis's scent. It headed to the south. We hadn't gone far when we discovered that the land beyond those ruins was being used as a dumpsite for all the shit that people couldn't bother taking to a hazardous waste disposal site. The ground positively reeked. And Davis, being a bright kid, had run right across that stinking ground, presuming one of his pursuers was still a werewolf.

Smart move, but it really didn't help the werewolves who were trying to save his ass. I walked all around the edge, but the area wasn't exactly small and by that point, my nose was so screwed up I could barely smell Clay standing two feet away.

We retraced our steps to the ruins. From there, we picked up Carter's scent. His trail ran straight and clear. Which would be so much better if he was the one I actually wanted to find.

"Follow it a little ways, darling," Clay said. "Maybe they met up. If not, maybe Malcolm can find Davis."

I nodded and texted Nick, asking him to take our tracking hound to the south and search for Davis's trail.

Carter had barely gone past the ruins and then, seeing nothing but desert, he'd circled toward the road. That seems clever—head for civilization—but to get there, he'd had to cut across open land, and he'd been spotted. His pursuers' trails resurfaced not far from his, heading in the same direction.

We were following the scents when Ruçi's phone buzzed in my pocket. I took it out to see that I'd missed a few texts. They'd started with polite inquiries as to his whereabouts. By this time, they'd escalated to: *Where the fuck are you? We need you here now! Got CC with the dart but lost him.*

I showed Clay. He frowned at the message.

"Dart?" he said.

"No idea. But if they're busy with Carter, I'm all for backing off and finding Davis. If Davis did loop back, though, and meet up…?"

Clay took the phone. He texted back. *Car accident. At motel now. Come here and we go together.*

Fuck you, was the reply.

"Good try," I said. If we could lure our targets somewhere, that would make our job a whole lot easier.

Clay texted. *Where are you?*

You're the fucking hound-dog. Find us. Over to the north.

Which didn't tell us anything we didn't know.

"I can keep trying," Clay said.

"And only risk tipping them off. Let's save that, make sure Davis isn't here and then…"

And then leave Carter to his fate. ⌐

Twenty-five

WE FOUND CARTER. He'd holed up on the roof of an auto-body shop, possibly the same one dumping those damned chemicals.

"About fucking time," he said when we climbed up.

"Where's Davis?" I asked.

"Who gives a shit?"

"I do," I said. "We've found you. You're fine. Now where is your cousin?"

"I'm *not* fine. They fucking shot me. Look."

He rubbed a bloody spot on the back of his shoulder. That's all it was—a spot of blood. From the dart, I presumed. Carter was sweating hard and shivering.

"It's a sedative," I said. "You're fine. Tell us where—"

"Fuck Davis. They shot me up with something. Now I'm sick, maybe dying..."

"Well, if you do, I'm sure your death won't be as bad as that girl's."

"What girl's?"

"The one you, Ford and Curtis held captive, raped, hunted, killed and ate."

"What?" His face screwed up, but he couldn't hide the *oh, shit* look deep in his eyes. "I don't know what you're talking—"

"She was a necromancer's daughter. Her ghost told her father what you did."

"Fuck! Necromancer? Seriously?" He stopped short. "What's a necromancer? I have no idea what you're talking about."

"Thanks for the confession."

"I never—" He seemed to realize he couldn't back out now and said, "It wasn't like that. She came onto me. Stalked me. Her daddy worked for one of those Cabals. He was doing research on werewolves, and he brought files home. She saw mine, with my photo and..." He shrugged. "She liked what she saw. She went to college near where I lived, so she tracked me down, pretended to bump into me at a bar, and asked me out. We got drunk, and she admitted she knew what I was, that she wanted to meet a werewolf. Wanted to screw a werewolf mostly. So if you're thinking she was some innocent little girl—"

"You held her captive."

"I had to, didn't I? She knew what I was. Yeah, I took her to a place we have in the woods. We had sex. Then I kept her there for a while."

"And called in Curtis and Ford to join the fun. And when you were done, you had a different kind of sport. Hunting and killing and eating—"

"She *knew* what we were. I couldn't let her live."

"Her father is a supernatural. That's not an exposure threat until *we* say it's an exposure threat. And no exposure threat ever warrants *rape*."

"It was her own damned fault. Stupid little slut. Any girl who goes into some deserted cabin with a strange guy for sex damned well deserves—"

I hit him. Just wheeled and punched, knocking him backward. Then I caught Clay's gaze, took a deep breath and motioned for him to take over.

"So that's why these guys came after you," he said. "You and Ford and Carter and Davis killed this girl—"

"Davis?" He sneered. "That pussy doesn't have the balls..." He stopped and cleared his throat. "Right. Yeah. Davis was there too, so there's no reason to go running off to save him. He's just as bad as the rest of us."

And that was the final proof we needed that Davis was, indeed, innocent of this.

I walked to the edge of the roof.

"You need to help me," Carter said. "I'm burning up and—" He hissed in pain and shoved up his shirtsleeve. His muscles were contorting, skin rippling, hairs poking through. "Shit. I'm Changing."

That explained the dart. It wasn't to sedate and slow him down but to force a Change.

Carter and Davis hadn't "escaped" the hotel. They were allowed to run in hopes they'd Change form to get away. Because the mercenaries couldn't bring back pelts if the boys didn't Change. This was the backup plan—a dart to force that transformation.

"You gotta help me," Carter said. "They're going to hunt and skin me. You're the Pack. You can't let them do that."

"No," I said. "We can't."

Clay had moved behind Carter. I knew what I had to do. And I hesitated. Clay didn't look my way, though. Didn't check for my signal. He reached down, grabbed Carter's head and snapped his neck. ⌒

Twenty-six

ICK TEXTED TO say they had Davis's trail, right as we were back on the trail of the mercenaries, having decided that made more sense. If we took them out, Davis would be safe. But when Nick sent that message, I paused, feeling the urge to switch to Davis's trail, protect him. I didn't look at Clay though. Didn't ask his opinion, as tempting as that was. I made the decision that my brain knew was right, even if it wasn't the one my gut wanted.

Stay on him, I sent back. *We'll follow mercs.*

I picked up the trail again, and we continued on. After a few minutes, I said, "I made a mistake."

"Following these guys? Hell, no. That's the logical—"

"I mean with Carter. I should have ordered his execution faster."

Clay waited as I crouched to recheck the trail. When I straightened, he said, "Did I look at you for a signal?"

"No, but—"

"Then there wouldn't have been any point in giving one. I knew what to do."

"I shouldn't have hesitated. The kid raped and murdered a girl. He's exactly the sort of werewolf we need to get rid of. Quickly. Before he gets older and worse."

"Doesn't matter what he'd done. You'd met him. Got to know him a little, and you might have thought he was a prick even before you found out what he did, but he was right in front of you. Ordering him to be killed while you watch? It's a helluva thing."

"Jeremy did it."

"Did he?" Clay glanced over. "How often was he standing in front of a mutt when he told me to finish him?"

"But he did. With Zack Cain and—"

"Very, very rarely, and if you think it was easy, you need to talk to him. That's one reason he stayed out of the field. Because he struggled to make the decisions that needed to be made, and he knew the best way to fix that was to not put himself in a situation where he'd see a kid like Carter and wonder if there was another way. There isn't. You know it. I know it. Jeremy would know it. A kid that rotten already isn't someone you can rehabilitate."

I nodded, did a sniff check and waved for us to veer east. "But you shouldn't have had to make that decision."

"There wasn't one to make. Just a sentence to carry out."

"Which isn't easy either. I don't want a free pass when you have to—"

He caught my arm and turned me to face him. "Which would you have rather done, darling? Snapped his neck yourself? Or ordered me to do it?"

Do it myself. There was no question, and when I didn't answer, he nodded and said, "Exactly. If I'd waited, you'd have made the only choice you could. It wasn't just an execution. It was a mercy killing. Which he probably didn't deserve, but like he said himself, we couldn't let those bastards skin him."

I nodded slowly. After a moment, I bent to the trail again. Ruçi's cell vibrated—I'd shut all the tones off. We'd decided against using the phone to lure them in, but if they initiated contact, we might be able to do it without making them suspicious. I took out the cell and read the text.

Where the fuck ARE you?

Out here, I replied. *Behind the motel. Where the fuck are YOU?*

You're the hound-dog. Use your nose.

Have you smelled the shit out here? Chemicals spilled everywhere. My nose is already fucked from that gas.

Fine. Sending you coordinates. You'd better remember how to use the GPS.

I check the installed GPS app. It was a high-tech one, showing the topography of the land, which made it easy to figure out where the mercenaries were. Out beyond the chemical dumpsite. Out in the desert.

"In the middle of nowhere," Clay murmured. "What did you warn those boys about? When your quarry heads off to a conveniently desolate place, perfect for a takedown…"

"It's not Fate smiling down. You've been made."

*

IT WAS NOT a guarantee that we had been made. But the possibility warned us to proceed with extreme caution. Ruçi's colleagues had begun to suspect something was up. Drawing him—or whoever had his phone—out into the open was their way of testing it.

We circled completely around the coordinates to come in the back way. The land was craggy enough for us to sneak up, but we were still fifty feet away from the rendezvous spot. Fifty feet away from a completely barren patch of desert. With no one in sight.

"What the hell?" Clay muttered. "Do they expect us to wander around there, staring at the GPS and going, 'Huh, this seems right,' so they can shoot us from a distance?"

"That or be absolutely sure it's Ruçi before they come out." I peered around. "Best spot to lie in wait with a gun?"

"Only spot is there." He nodded toward a scrubby patch of bushes.

"Then they aren't exactly experienced snipers, are they?"

He frowned. I told him what I had in mind, and then I set out. If they were waiting for whoever had Ruçi's phone to come wandering out, GPS in hand, I gave them exactly that. I just did it by wandering in from the west—straight from the direction of the late-afternoon sun, huge and bright as it dropped toward the horizon.

I was still careful, in case they weren't as sun-blinded as I hoped. I kept my ears attuned for any sound as my gaze returned to that patch of bushes, watching for the first sign of movement inside. I zigzagged, too, holding up the phone, as if trying to match my position with the coordinates.

Sometimes, I really appreciate being a blonde. No one thinks anything of it if you act like a ditz. Less than five minutes later, I heard the sound I'd been listening for. The *oomph* and gasp of a surprise attack, as Clay crept in from the other direction. A shot fired, and my stomach seized at that, but a heartbeat later, Clay yelled, "Clear!"

I broke into a run and made it to the bushes just as a guy came flying out of them, airborne. I pounced on him. It was an easy takedown. I think he was still in shock. Unexpected werewolf attacks do that to people.

I pinned him and patted him down as a grunt and a yowl sounded from the bushes. The other guy sailed out, with Clay running out after him. He pinned the man and patted him for weapons.

The two mercenaries didn't say a word during any of this. They managed a few remarkably wolf-like snarls, but that's just because they were pissed off at themselves for being taken. They were professionals—they wouldn't beg for mercy or spit idle threats.

I'd taken a cell phone, knife and wallet from my guy when his phone buzzed with an incoming message. I checked it.

You find the bitch with the phone yet? Ruçi has DC's trail. Leaving the bitch and CC to you.

Clay caught my expression. I said nothing, just grabbed a few of Vanessa's cuff-ties from my pocket and threw him two. The moment we had our guys bound hand and foot, we were off.

The mercenaries had brought in reinforcements to replace their lost men after all. And those reinforcements had gone to check on Ruçi when he didn't answer some of their texts. They'd found him, freed him and brought him here while Clay had been texting about a "car accident," confirming that we had Ruçi's phone.

We'd thought that phone was a good way to lure them in. They'd thought the same about us.

I'd texted Nick before I even put the cuffs on my downed guy. They were on Davis's trail. Hopefully, closer than Ruçi.

Vanessa sent me the coordinates of their current location and kept me updated. We were a few hundred feet out when I smelled Ruçi and at least one stranger. Again, I paused to consider my next move. Again, I knew what it had to be. Trust that Nick and Vanessa were closing in on Davis, and go after these guys instead.

We'd jogged maybe fifty more feet, when Clay said, "Hold up," and dropped to one knee. He pointed at the ground. It was a sandy patch over rock. On it, I could see paw prints. I bent to sniff, just to be sure, and nodded.

"Ruçi," I said.

"He's Changed form."

"Probably caught a whiff of all our scents back at the motel and realized he was safer as a wolf."

We picked up speed. I'd have loved to Change myself, but it wasn't long before I could smell the humans in the wind. Two of them.

Another quick assessment. Another decision led by my brain and not my gut. Forget the werewolf. Stick to the guys with guns. For us, they were a lot more dangerous out here in this open land.

We tracked them down quickly enough. Again the desert robbed us of an easy way to sneak up, but we accommodated with a variation on our last trick. This time, Clay played decoy, running doubled over through a patch of cacti and making only enough noise to get their attention without causing them to suspect a trap.

They'd just raised their guns when I attacked from the rear. I grabbed the one guy's arm while kicking the other. I didn't quite manage to knock the second guy down—my trajectory was a little off—but I had the added element of "we're being attacked by a woman" surprise, which is almost as good as the werewolf-attack one. The first guy dropped his gun the moment I wrenched his arm. I knocked it skidding away. The other caught my second kick—this one in the gut—before he could swing his gun around.

I jumped on the second guy to disarm him. He countered with a kick of his own, one that hit me square in the shin with his steel-toed boots, and there was a split-second of blinding pain before I recovered and pinned him. I was grabbing his gun when I saw the first guy running for his. I lunged, but that moment of pain-blinded hesitation had been one moment too much. There was no way I could take down the first guy before he got to his gun. And Clay was too far to do it for me.

The guy dove for the gun. I leaped, hoping to knock him down before he had time to aim. Before I could, he spun and toppled to the ground. Which made a lot more sense when

I saw blood blossoming on his shoulder and looked to see Vanessa running our way with her gun raised.

We were wordlessly tying up the two mercenaries when Ruçi's scent drifted over on the breeze. Clay caught it a split-second later. Then Davis's smell came from the same direction.

We were off and running, leaving Vanessa to finish the binding. A moment later, I heard her right behind us. That's when we crested a rise and spotted Davis. He was about two hundred feet away, sitting in front of a small grouping of cacti.

"What the hell is he...?" Clay began.

He didn't finish. In the time it took to say that much, we'd gotten close enough to make out blood on Davis's shirt, and I could see his head dropped forward, his chest heaving, his breath coming so hard I could hear it.

"Dart," I said. "He's Changing."

"Yeah, but not fast enough for that."

Clay pointed to the side, and I saw a blond wolf creeping Davis's way. The boy was too far gone to notice. Also too far gone to defend himself. And we were still a good hundred feet out. Ruçi seemed to be taking his time, though. Waiting the Change out. Which meant—

I skidded to a halt before Ruçi spotted us, but I was too late. He saw us coming and charged. Davis heard that. He was already starting his Change, but he managed to push up and stagger a few steps. Ruçi was closing in and there was no way Clay and I could make it—

A black streak shot from the right. Malcolm, running full out toward Davis and Ruçi. The Albanian had been about to spring when he saw Malcolm, and that was just enough to make him abort his leap. Davis kept stumbling out of the way. Malcolm zoomed past him and barreled into Ruçi.

Malcolm and Ruçi went down in a blur of yellow and black fur, snarling and snapping. Nick came running and stood there, monitoring the fight while Clay and I went to Davis, helped him to his feet and got him as far away as he could manage before he started convulsing, the Change coming hard. Then, as Vanessa stood guard with her gun, I told Davis it was safe, everyone was accounted for, he should just Change and get it over with. Clay helped him out of his torn clothing as I talked. Then I left them, Clay watching over him as I hurried back to where Malcolm was battling Ruçi.

As fights went, it wasn't nearly on the caliber of Clay's bout with Malcolm. Ruçi might have been a skilled mercenary, but he wasn't a top-notch fighter. As he'd said, he worked mostly with other supernaturals, which may have meant he had little experience with wolf-on-wolf fighting.

By now, Malcolm should have won handily. But he didn't seem to be giving it his all. Was he still hurt from his bout with Clay? Had he hidden serious injuries out of pride? He didn't look wounded, though. Just not fighting at full strength. Finally, when Ruçi seemed ready to just drop from exhaustion, Malcolm snorted, as if in disgust, and took him down, pinning him with his jaws around the mutt's neck.

Ruçi deflated, his flanks heaving in a sigh, like a prizefighter acknowledging a takedown. As if he expected to just rise and walk away. Malcolm pulled back for the killing blow. Then he glanced at me.

It didn't matter if Ruçi's crimes weren't as bad as Carter's. Didn't matter if he was just a hired gun. He was a werewolf who'd taken a job to hunt and skin fellow werewolves. The punishment was as clear as it would have been for Carter. And with Malcolm watching, I could not hesitate.

I nodded, and Malcolm ripped out Ruçi's throat. ⌒

Twenty-seven

WE HAD SOME cleanup work to do before we left. The guys and Vanessa tackled that while I took care of Davis. He'd managed to fully Change, but the dart left him too sick to do more than lie on his side as a wolf, shivering. After a half-hour, as his shaking subsided, I asked him to try Changing back. It took a while, but he managed it. Then we sat there, in the desert, him huddled with his knees up, arms wrapped around them, trying to keep the tattered remains of his jeans in place.

He asked if I knew why they'd done this to his family. I told him. As horrible as it was, he had to know.

As I finished, he started shivering again.

"I...I remember that." His gaze shot my way. "Not that I knew what they'd done. If I did..."

He swallowed. "A few months ago, Curtis went to hang out with Ford and Carter. A last-minute thing. He wanted me to come. He said Carter had this girl who liked to party with werewolves, and Carter didn't mind sharing her. I said I was busy working, but the truth is that I just…I didn't want a girl like that, passing her around with my cousins. I thought that's what it was. That she was, you know, into it. It never occurred to me that she wasn't, and maybe it should have, because Curtis used to make comments about hooking me up with girls, guaranteed…" He glanced at me, color rising in his cheeks. "Well, you know."

"Guaranteed scores."

"Yeah, and honestly, I figured they were like hookers. The kind of girls you don't actually pay, but you bring a couple of bottles or leave them some 'rent' money. I wasn't interested. But now I'm thinking maybe he meant…well, something else."

"Maybe."

"Still…and I'm not cutting Curtis any slack here. Anything he did was unforgivable. But I remember he came home after that visit, and he took me aside, and he said to stay away from Carter. He looked sick when he said it. Told me Carter was a fucked-up bastard and made me promise to keep as far away from him as I could. I said I would—it wasn't like Carter and I got along anyway."

Which suggested it hadn't been three psychopathic Cains responsible for this atrocity. Yes, Ford and Curtis had gone to that cabin. Yes, they'd had sex with the girl. Maybe Carter had her drunk enough that she didn't fight, but there was no way in hell the guys wouldn't have realized she wasn't exactly in any shape to consent. That was their crime. Had they helped hunt and kill her? Or was that just Carter? Or had he engineered it—maybe forcing her to "escape" so she had to be taken down. I don't know. I'll never know.

I did know that I couldn't let the man who'd engineered this get away scot-free. I understood why he'd gone after the werewolves who'd horribly murdered his daughter. If Carter had been the only one he'd targeted, I wasn't sure what I'd do. But it hadn't just been Carter. It'd been two werewolves whose level of participation remained unclear. And three others who'd played absolutely no role in her death. As Alpha, I would need to deal with that.

*

WE SPLIT UP for the trip to the airport—Malcolm was with Clay and me. It was a quiet drive for about ten minutes. Then Malcolm said, "Not even going to acknowledge what I did, are you?"

"And what would that be?" I asked.

He snorted. "So that's how we're going to play it? I put my life on the line for some mutt kid and you're all going to pretend it never happened? Just keep telling me what a selfish asshole I am."

"Put your life on the line?" Clay said. "If Davis hadn't been drugged, even he could have taken that guy down."

"Which I didn't know when I leapt in, did I?" Malcolm said. "He was supposed to be a hard-assed mercenary. I expected a real fight."

"Exactly," I said. "You expected a real fight. Maybe not with the odds so heavily in his favor that your death was guaranteed, but a good enough fight. A good enough opponent. A worthy opponent. A worthy death."

"What?"

"Death by mutt," Clay said. "For thirty years, we believed the story that when you left Stonehaven, you went out looking for a good death. Challenging mutts until you found one who could kill you. You let the story go out that you had, but either you couldn't find anyone good enough or you changed your mind. Now, as you begin what is guaranteed to be a downhill road, that's what you're looking for again. A Pack werewolf's death."

"That why you seemed disappointed in Bulgaria," I said, "when I didn't really set Clay on you. That would have been a good death. At Clay's hands, on my order, both having betrayed you. Lends a little much-needed nobility to your demise. That's why you won't just provoke me into ordering your death. *Righteous* execution by the Pack *really* isn't what you have in mind for your end."

"This is why you wanted back in," Clay said. "You don't want protection. You want exactly what you said—to protect *us*. Not because you give a shit about us, but because this is how you want to die. As you once lived. Doing the one job that, at least to you, had some honor. Being the Pack's enforcer. You told Elena that's your role here, that she can send you on any mission. That you will be the best weapon we could ask for. The best protector for our children. Which you are. A werewolf who truly is not afraid to die."

Silence stretched for at least twenty seconds. Then Malcolm said, "Is that such a bad thing?"

"No," I said. "If you're offering to be the expendable muscle in this Pack, then I accept that offer. You'll get your honorable death, Malcolm, even if you don't deserve it, because you owe the Pack and this is how you will repay us. You will take every job I give you, even if there's no chance you'll get that honorable death doing it."

"I understand that. Whatever you might think of me, Elena, I'm here for more than a good death. There was no guarantee that mutt today could do the job. I still saved that boy. I did my duty. As a Pack wolf."

"And you will continue to do it. Also, in your quest for that warrior's death, if you ever endanger anyone in my Pack—"

"I won't. That would defeat the purpose."

"Then you'll get what you want. On one last condition."

"Which is?"

"Shut the fuck up." Clay twisted in the passenger seat to face him. "You don't like us? You don't respect us? The feeling is mutual, but you are Pack now, so we won't snipe at you. And you'll do the same for us or you won't get what you want, because you won't be Pack anymore. Understood?"

A long silence. Then, "Understood." ⌐

Twenty-eight

WE PUT MALCOLM on a flight to Pittsburgh. Then we flew to Cincinnati to get our cars. After the long drive back, we spent the night at the Sorrentinos'. Clay and I may also have slept in. Or not really "slept" so much as "didn't leave bed until almost noon." Even then we only got up because someone wouldn't stop banging on the guest house door.

It was Nick. "Yes, I dropped off breakfast. That wasn't an invitation to stay in here all day."

"Nah," Clay said. "We'd need lunch for that." He checked his watch.

"There's food in the main house. That's what I came to get you for. That, and to get you the hell out of my guest house so I can get the sheets changed for tonight."

"Davis decided to stay?" I said as we walked toward the house.

"For now. Poor kid doesn't really have anywhere else to go. There are relatives, but those bastards wiped out every Cain he was close to. I'm giving him Morgan's room. The guest house is for Vanessa and me. Give her some privacy and..." He motioned between the main house and the guest one. "Give *us* privacy, as you can see. It's just the right distance that even werewolf hearing can't pick up any sounds."

"So she's moving in."

"She is. After Sophie graduates in the spring. I'm going to do some remodeling in the guest house. Maybe put on an addition. Not really a home for us but..." He shrugged. "Moving in that direction."

"You've got lots of land if you ever want to move further in that direction."

He smiled. "I know. I'm already planning. I'm just not telling her that yet. I don't want to scare her off."

I hugged him. "I don't think that's possible. Congratulations."

We went inside, where everyone was in the dining room, milling about, waiting to eat. Vanessa was talking to Antonio. Davis was listening to Reese and Noah explain the post-secondary school options in the area.

"Yeah, I'd like to go back," Davis was saying. "I don't know if I can still get my football scholarship—I kinda bailed midterm, but I've saved up some money from working." He glanced at me. "Not that I'm going to jump and enroll at a New York college. I'm not, well, I don't know…"

"You've had a lot happen very quickly," I said. "You couldn't enroll until fall anyway. So slow down, take some time and figure out what you want. In the meantime, if you'd like a job…"

"I would. Definitely. I'm not…I don't want to…you know, impose…"

"Antonio always has work—temporary or otherwise—at his company. There's no rush and no pressure. No obligation either. Just relax for a while."

He exhaled. "I will. Thanks."

"And I hear you're staying on soon, too?" I said to Vanessa.

She smiled. "I am. Playing Wendy to the lost boys. Just as long as they don't expect me to take over the housekeeping."

"No," Noah said. "But I was hoping for more lessons at the gun range."

"That I can do. And split cooking duties with Reese." She turned to Davis. "Do you like baklava?"

He smiled. "I like food, whatever it is."

"Spoken like a true werewolf. Okay then, gang, dig— Wait. Sorry. Werewolf household. Werewolf rules." She turned and held out a plate. "Alpha first."

I took the plate and dove in. Sometimes, it's good to be Alpha.

And sometimes, it really isn't, not when you need to do things to your Pack that you would give anything to avoid—like bringing in the guy who'd tried to ruin their lives. But Malcolm wasn't a danger to them anymore, and he *was* an invaluable weapon. That rationale still didn't make it easy. It was a choice, though. A choice that they endorsed.

Maybe what it came down to isn't that I'd summoned the demon who tormented them, but that in bringing this demon back, I gave them the chance to exorcise him, to turn him into an ordinary man, an old wolf just looking for a place to die. And if I've done that for them, then it's worth it. It really is.